A STITCH IN CRIME

A HATTI LEHTINEN MYSTERY

A STITCH IN CRIME

ANN YOST

FIVE STAR
A part of Gale, Cengage Learning

GALE
CENGAGE Learning

Farmington Hills, Mich • San Francisco • New York • Waterville, Maine
Meriden, Conn • Mason, Ohio • Chicago

LIBRARY OF CONGRESS CATALOGING-IN-PUBLICATION DATA

Yost, Ann.
 A stitch in crime : a Hatti Lehtinen mystery / Ann Yost. — First edition.
  pages cm.
 ISBN 978-1-4328-3042-7 (hardcover) — ISBN 1-4328-3042-2 (hardcover) — ISBN 978-1-4328-3029-8 (ebook) — 1-4328-3029-5 (ebook)
 1. Women police chiefs—Fiction. 2. Knitters—Fiction. 3. Murder—Investigation—Fiction. I. Title.
PS3625.O7585S85 2015
813'.6—dc23   2014041558

First Edition. First Printing: April 2015
Find us on Facebook– https://www.facebook.com/FiveStarCengage
Visit our website– http://www.gale.cengage.com/fivestar/
Contact Five Star™ Publishing at FiveStar@cengage.com

Printed in the United States of America
1 2 3 4 5 6 7 19 18 17 16 15

To Adam, Cathy and Julian

CHAPTER ONE

The annual St. Lucy's Day parade was about to start and, at least crime-wise, all was quiet on the Northern front, which might seem like an odd thing to be grateful for, but then, I am, at the moment, the sole representative of what passes for the law in my hometown, Red Jacket, Michigan.

Not that we ever have much in the way of burglary or murder. There's not much to steal in our time-capsule community located on the Keweenaw Peninsula, a witch's finger of land that crooks into frigid Lake Superior.

And then there's the weather; as one wag puts it, "there are two seasons on the Keweenaw, swattin' and shovelin'." Today, December thirteenth, there was a foot of snow on the ground, and it continued to fall.

But back to the subject of crime. For the past week, I, as temporary, acting police chief, had fielded daily complaints about our latest controversy, Arvo Maki's unfortunate choice for this year's St. Lucy, and I hoped to survive the event and get back to the challenge of emptying frozen parking meters. Oh, and to running my shop, a hybrid fishing-slash-knitting shop called Bait & Stitch.

That hope died as my front door banged open and the welcoming bell instead of tinkling sweetly, clanged harshly, let go its moorings and flew across the shop. Ronja Laplander, as short and squat as one of the rock houses left over from the long-gone days of copper mining, steamed across my linoleum

7

floor with all the grace of a bottom-heavy freighter making its way through the Soo Locks. Her fists disappeared into the folds of flesh at her waist, and the straight bangs of her dark brown hair that ended an inch above her unibrow lifted with each heavy breath.

"I want to register a complaint, Hatti."

"Again?"

Ronja ignored my obvious lack of interest as she had every day since Arvo had taken it upon himself to unilaterally name Liisa Pelonen as this year's St. Lucy. Silently, I mouthed the words with her.

"Arvo had no right to choose that outsider."

It wasn't that I didn't sympathize with Ronja. Arvo Maki is the owner of our only funeral home, which, in a region with a skyrocketing aging index, explains much of his wealth and standing. He is the de facto mayor, head of the chamber of commerce, self-appointed cheerleader and godfather for our financially struggling town, and he is used to getting his own way. This time, though, he'd gone too far. He'd tampered with tradition in bypassing the traditional St. Lucy vote and unilaterally appointing his protégé to the coveted role. It didn't matter that Liisa was a stunningly lovely blue-eyed blonde, perfect for the part. She was a newcomer. She'd line jumped. I nodded at Ronja.

"Duly noted."

The angry woman ignored me as she whipped herself into a frenzy.

"He should be strung up by his thumbs. He should be boiled in oil. He should be murdered." Her volume, already at a dangerous level, increased several decibels with each suggestion. "He should be murdered, Hatti," she repeated with a death-inducing glare. "And that girl, too. She should be murdered, too."

Ronja hadn't mentioned murder before. I sensed the situation was spiraling out of control, and I thought I knew why. In a few minutes everyone in town would watch Liisa Pelonen, clad in the martyr's white robe, scarlet sash and crown of candles, driven down Main Street in the back of Ollie Rahkonen's sleigh.

Ronja firmly believed that it was Astrid Laplander's turn to try to balance on the rickety, wooden sleigh, to inhale the pungent scent of Claude, Ollie's gassy reindeer, and to turn into a human Popsicle. Astrid, Ronja's eldest daughter. Not Liisa Pelonen, a refugee from Ahmeek, some ten miles to the north, who had lived in Red Jacket for only six months, as a guest at the funeral home.

"Well, Hatti? What are you going to do about it?"

It was a ridiculous question. There was nothing I could do about it. There never had been. No one in Red Jacket ever second-guessed Arvo. Not my stepdad, his best friend. Not the temporary, acting police chief, me. Not even his own wife. I glanced behind me, belatedly remembering that said wife, Pauline Maki, had been making a purchase at the cash register when Ronja blustered through the door. Pauline, unfazed, stepped forward.

"I'm so sorry Arvo's decision upset you," she said. I heard the genuine sympathy in her voice. "He meant no disrespect, but, in the excitement of getting ready for the festival and the visiting members of the tourist council, he simply forgot about protocol."

I gazed in admiration at the funeral director's wife. Pauline was not just a master of diplomacy, she was a genius. In her sincere apology she'd managed to include a reference to the economic stakes involved in the St. Lucy parade and the weekend's festival. This year's festival was designed to bolster our tourist trade, an issue of paramount importance to Ronja, whose family owned the Copper Kettle, a gift shop down the block. Since the closing of the copper mines and the departure of the logging industry, tourism was our life's blood. Arvo, whose *raison d'être* was Red Jacket's economic survival, had cooked up *Pikkujoulu,* which means "Little Christmas," in the hope of getting the state tourist council to give our town a station on the proposed Keweenaw Snow Train. The Snow Train would, we hoped, bring tourists to the Upper Peninsula during the long, snow-filled winters.

I half-listened to Pauline's soothing voice as I rang up her purchase, a skein of hand-painted, coral, merino wool, so I knew the exact moment the appeasement strategy went off the rails.

"Perhaps your daughter—Astrid, is it?—could be St. Lucy next year."

The suggestion would sound perfectly reasonable to an outsider. Pauline, who had lived here for twenty-five years, still didn't understand the ridiculous amount of importance laid on the title. The girls in the Finnish Lutheran community and, more importantly, their mothers, coveted the honor of playing St. Lucy. It was equivalent to head cheerleader in Texas or prom queen in any high school in America. It was better than National Merit Scholar or student council president or winning a Rhodes scholarship. The opportunity to wear the crown of candles launched a girl into a life of success, which, on the Keweenaw, mostly meant marriage to someone capable of finding and holding a job. It was the Holy Grail.

"Next year," Ronja shouted at the taller woman, "is for Valentina. After that is Katrina, then Olga, then Vesta." And then, just as I was wondering what on earth made Ronja think all five of her very plain daughters would have been elected St. Lucy, she delivered the sucker punch. "You would understand if you had a daughter of your own."

Pauline did not move a millimeter, but under the carefully

applied makeup, her face was the color of rice paper. I was furious.

"Geez Louise." I grabbed Ronja's sausage-like arm and steered her toward the door. "Your beef is with Arvo. The next time you want to complain, go to him." I opened the door hard enough to make the little bell shriek, if it had still been attached, and came face-to-face with my sister, Sofi Teljo, and my assistant, Einar Eino, both of whom looked startled.

"Pardon me," I said, firmly, "Ronja was just leaving." Sofi, always quick to grasp a situation, took Ronja's other arm, and together we deposited her on the sidewalk before returning to the shop. I had no idea what to say to Pauline, who continued to stand, white-faced and silent, a mechanical smile on her face. "I'm so sorry." I knew the words were inadequate.

"Don't give it a thought," she said, finally. "Mrs. Laplander is perfectly right. Arvo shouldn't have interfered with tradition. It was just that Liisa seemed so perfect for St. Lucy. And, of course, we are so attached to her. She has become like a surrogate daughter to us. I'll make sure their daughter has a role in the mid-winter festival."

It would be an empty gesture. No part in Heikinpäivä could compete with the honor of portraying St. Lucy.

"I'd better scoot," Pauline said, apparently recovered from the attack. At least the color had returned to her cheeks. "Arvo's got the tourist council members over on the reviewing stand."

I glanced out my plate-glass window, in between the Glass-Wax–stenciled snowflakes, to catch a glimpse of Arvo: tall, fit and Scandinavian-handsome with his ruddy cheeks and silver-white hair. He was holding forth to a trio of men whose Burberry topcoats and cashmere scarves marked them as out-of-towners among the plaid hunting jackets, parkas and winter kromers, a cap with earflaps that is manufactured in Ironwood and much beloved on the Keweenaw.

"The trouble is," Sofi said, as soon as the door closed behind Arvo's wife, "the Makis have made too much of Liisa. They started out offering her a room to use while she finishes up at Copper County High, but they treat her like a daughter. Arvo, in particular, has gone off the deep end on this surrogate parenting thing."

"It's the novelty of the experience," I said thoughtfully. "It can't have been easy being childless in a town that's as family obsessed as this one." I gazed at my sister, who was wearing a waist-length wig of red hair and an ancient bathrobe adorned with glued-on feathers. "You look just like the pictures of Louhi."

"Bah." Einar, who had resumed his seat on the high stool near the counter, a position he occupied for close to eight hours a day, every day, gifted us with a few carefully chosen words on one of his pet topics. "You don't get no husband in dat. No man want witch."

"You know Arvo asked us to dress as characters from the Kalevala," Sofi explained, "and I shouldn't have to remind you that I don't want another husband."

I couldn't help thinking that Einar himself, without the benefit of a costume, looked exactly like a tonttu, a gnome-like creature from the pages of Finnish mythology. He was short and billiard-ball-bald with bright blue eyes, and, when he chose to share it, an oddly sweet smile. I'd inherited him from my stepdad, along with the shop, and, to be perfectly frank, I couldn't imagine how I'd operate without him. Einar knew everything there was to know about fishing, he tied masses of intricate flies and, most importantly, he handled the live bait.

Sofi's voice faded as I hurried into the narrow stockroom at the back of my rectangular shop and struggled into my own costume, a gold, spray-painted Hotpoint box. I was the Magic

Sampo, a mill that could turn anything into gold, and I'd thought it was a clever costume until I got a hint of the spatial problems I was facing. On my way out of the room I bumped into a shelf and knocked a gross of fish hooks onto the floor, but there was no time to pick them up. Sofi and I were nearly late as it was.

"*Voi*, Henrikki," Einar said when he saw me. "You not get husband neither wearing a box. Poys like curves."

"Hatti isn't in the market for a new husband," Sofi reminded the old man. "Remember? She's still married."

"Temporarily married." I was anxious to change the subject, and I smiled at Einar. "Will you come to the parade with us?"

He shook his head. "*Ei*. I go sauna." He pronounced it sow-na, in the approved Yooper way. Sauna is an integral part of our subculture, a ritual so ubiquitous that every home, no matter how poor, has its own personal bath house.

"Lucky you," I said, meaning it. I asked him to lock up as my sister and I stepped out into a blaze of illumination created by the thousands of tiny twinkle lights that crisscrossed Main Street. There were wreaths and bows in all the windows and on the lamp posts. A banner taller than my fifteen-year-old niece, Charlie, was stretched across the second story of Hakala's Pharmacy. It shouted: Welcome to *Pikkujoulu*!

"It looks like the Christmas Fairy threw up around here."

"The Finnish Christmas Fairy," Sofi corrected me. "When was the last time we had this many folks on Main Street?"

"Nineteen ten."

It was a popular joke in Red Jacket, whose copper mining heyday had begun in the late nineteenth century and ended more than fifty years ago. Main Street, in fact the whole town, was unusually opulent for a rural outpost because the copper barons had had more money than they knew what to do with. The stretch of three-story buildings on Main Street was

13

constructed with Jacobsville sandstone. They boasted turrets, columns and an occasional gargoyle. A pair of Gothic cathedrals, St. Heikki's and St. Anne's, guarded opposite ends of the small town like a pair of medieval dragons. We even had an ornate theater called the Opera House. But the wear and tear of a century, combined with our persistently lean times, had taken a toll, and the bricks were stained, the facades, grimy. To outside eyes, the town appeared worn out. Snow softened the shabbiness, which was fortunate, as our yearly snowfall averages two hundred inches.

I felt my usual twinge of affection for and worry about the people of Red Jacket.

"Do you think *Pikkujoulu* will catch on?"

Sofi is seven years older than my twenty-eight years, shorter, softer and prettier despite added softness to her jowls and the new lines in her face thanks to her three-year-old divorce. Perhaps because of that divorce, she's developed a streak of cynicism. She shook her head.

"This has 'one-hit wonder' written all over it. Face it, Hatti. There's a perfectly good Bavarian-themed Christmas Festival down in Frankenmuth with all-you-can-eat-fried chicken. Who in their right mind would drive an additional ten hours for smorgasbord and St. Lucy?"

"And snow. We've always got snow." I stuck out my tongue and caught a drifting snowflake on it as we walked up Main Street and listened to a canned version of a Finnish carol, "Hanki, Hanki, Hanki" ("Snow, Snow, Snow"), on the outdoor sound system Arvo had rigged up. Suddenly the music stopped, and, a moment later, we heard the familiar strains of Santa Lucia and watched as Claude began to slip and slide his way down Main Street's slight incline. Liisa, transcendently beautiful despite her thin white robe and the electric crown of candles, waved at the folks lining the sidewalks. I couldn't help noticing she wasn't smiling.

"She does look like the perfect St. Lucy," I admitted, admiring her thick, wheat-colored braids, clear blue eyes and delicate features. Liisa, like my sister and me, was descended from the Swedish Finns and not the reindeer-herding Samis who came from the Arctic Circle.

After the sleigh passed us, we fell in behind it with our fellow costumed merchants and the boys and girls, who wore cone-shaped hats, waved star-topped wands and carried lighted candles. At the bottom of Main Street we turned west down Pine, stopping when we arrived at the Old Finnish Cemetery. The children rolled snowballs to prop their lighted candles next to the ancient headstones, and I felt again that tightening in my throat. I'd always loved our custom of including the departed in our holiday observances.

Afterwards, we headed for home, retracing our steps up Main Street, then walking an additional two blocks to Calumet Street, where I was currently living in our yellow-sided Queen Anne–style family home. Sofi and Charlie lived across the street in a duplex shared with our great aunt Ianthe and her companion, Miss Irene Suutala.

"You've been back for a year now," Sofi said, in what she probably hoped was a casual tone. "Made any decisions yet?"

"Well, I know for sure I don't ever want to become a real cop."

I'd taken over for our stepdad, Carl Lehtinen—whom we called Pops—after he was injured in a hit-and-run snowmobile accident in November. It had been Arvo's idea. He'd said that Copper County Sheriff Horace Clump had been pressuring the town council to sign a contract for law enforcement services and that Pops's recuperation at the Mayo Clinic left a crack into which Clump would try to slither. Privately, I questioned whether Clump, built like Humpty-Dumpty with no discernible neck and most of his weight around the middle, would be able to slither into anything, but I took Arvo's point. I could save Pops's job, and the town's police department, by barely lifting a finger. After all, there's never any serious crime on the Keweenaw.

"What about the shop?"

"What's not to like about Bait & Stitch? Einar handles the slimy work. All I have to do is stock and sell yarn and schedule meetings of the knitting circle, and you know how much I love that."

The Keweenaw Knitters included Sofi and me, our cousin Elli Risto, who is the owner of the Leaping Deer Bed & Breakfast and my lifelong best friend, and Sonya Stillwater, a Navajo midwife who'd relocated from the southwest.

"I know you love the circle. What about your marriage?"

I was prepared for the question. I knew I'd freaked out my family when I'd left the world's shortest marriage to return to Red Jacket in a body bag. I'd finally told them a little about the blow-up but not much, mostly because I still didn't understand it myself. One day we were married and (I thought) happy as clams, and the next Jace was telling me it was over. I hadn't seen him or talked to him in a year.

"Time to throw in the towel," I said, in an attempt at a lightness I didn't feel. "Once we're *Pikkujoulu*-ed out, I'm going to file for divorce."

"I'm sorry, Hatti."

I waved a dismissive hand. "It's no big deal. The same thing happened to you."

But it hadn't been the same thing. Sofi's marriage had exploded due to cheating. Mine had just disappeared, like the populations of the ghost towns that litter the Keweenaw. Marriage canceled due to lack of interest. I still didn't understand, but I knew it was time to move on.

"We're glad to have you home, honey," my sister said, attempting to hug me around my soggy costume. "I'm glad to have you home."

I nodded, a little choked up.

"I realize that, compared with the nation's capital, there's not much excitement here on the Keweenaw."

"I don't know. I could stand on Pennsylvania Avenue every day for years and I'd never get to see a St. Lucy's Day parade."

Sofi laughed, but the grin soon disappeared.

"Sofe," I said, "I'm a little worried about Ronja. Just before you came into the shop she was issuing death threats about Arvo and Liisa. I've seen that woman angry before—we all have—but not like this."

Sofi nodded. "Hell hath no fury. But I don't think you need to fret anymore. St. Lucy's Day is almost over, and, secondly, murder just isn't in our culture. The last violent death in Red Jacket was before the millennium, unless you count the suicidal deer that keep flinging themselves at the vehicles on M-41. Ronja may be angry, but she's not a fool. On some level, she knows that playing St. Lucy is not a matter of life and death."

"I hope you're right," I said, somewhat comforted. "I've still got a week as top cop."

CHAPTER TWO

Larry, my parents' middle-aged basset hound, was too well-bred to be overly demonstrative, but I could tell he was glad to see me. Or maybe he was just relieved. After all, it was well past his supper time.

"The parade ran long," I apologized, "and Ronja Laplander kicked up another fuss about St. Lucy. Geez Louise. If she thought she could get away with it, I think she really would kill Arvo and Liisa, too."

I couldn't help noticing Larry didn't look all that impressed with my account of Ronja's hyperbolic rage. Of course, he'd heard versions of the same tale every day all week. I peeled off what was left of the wet cardboard, then filled his bowl with kibble and topped it with a couple of mea culpa scrambled eggs. After he'd eaten, I buried my fingertips in the soft fur behind his ears. His eyes rolled upwards and his lashes dropped, and I knew I was forgiven. When the mantel clock in the parlor chimed six times, I realized that, while I desperately needed a shower thanks to the combination of snow and sweat that had plastered my hair to my head and my clothes to my skin, there wasn't time to take one; I was already late for the smorgasbord at the B&B scheduled for the pleasure and feeding of the out-of-town guests, and I was supposed to help with the serving. I'd have to use my fallback plan of volunteering to dish out the odiferous vinegar cabbage that was Edna Moilanen's signature dish.

I raced up the polished walnut staircase, darted into my bedroom and threw on my standard ethnic costume: a long-sleeved white blouse fastened at the neck with a golden Solje pin, an embroidered vest that my mother had worn during her brief flirtation with a kantele group and a plaid kilt left over from high-school field hockey. Sofi called it my lonely goat-herdess outfit. I hurried back downstairs, thrust my bare feet into a pair of snow boots, threw on an ancient pink parka, then waded through the foot-and-a-half of virgin snow that covered our yards, mine and Elli's.

The inn had been built more than a hundred years earlier for the manager of the Toivo mine and his large family. It was a rambling Edwardian structure that my uncle, Kuusta Risto, had inherited from his family. He and my mother's sister had operated the Dew Drop Inn for decades. The decrease in tourists due to the state's long economic downturn, combined with a sharp spike in gas prices, eventually added up to very little business. My aunt and uncle retired to Florida, leaving the ramshackle structure in the hands of their daughter.

Elli is a dynamo in the guise of a pixie. She has enormous blue-green eyes and strawberry blond curls, and her insane energy level is only surpassed in intensity by her warm heart. Elli had spent the last few years rehabilitating the place to its former glory with structural changes and a hard-target search of flea markets and antique shops. Her greatest points of pride were the three-story walnut grand staircase, the stained glass side panels in the front window and the elephant hide wallpaper in the dining room. It was a masterful job, and, aside from the wallpaper, which I considered a little creepy, I only took issue with her choice of a name: The Leaping Deer.

"I'm afraid it will remind people of all those carcasses out on M-41," I'd pointed out. But it was too late. I'd been in Washington, D.C., when she'd been considering her options,

and Arvo, liking the image of a leaping deer, had used all his charm and leverage to influence Elli's decision.

As I mounted the shoveled steps to the wraparound front porch, I reflected that the inn's name was yet another example of Arvo's heavy-handedness. Even so, I knew he meant well.

The front door stood open, and Arvo was standing in the foyer, apparently waiting for me. Speak of the devil. He gave me a big hug.

"Hatti-girl! *Hyvää Joulua!*"

Arvo tended to lapse into Finnish when he was excited or emotional. Or both. He beamed at me, his wide, handsome face glowing with happiness above a bright red Christmas sweater that he wore over a white, silk shirt. His impeccably tailored charcoal slacks looked crisp and clean despite his hours outside in the falling snow, and his crystal blue eyes sparkled at me until they focused on the area just under my chin. The smile dimmed and a furrow appeared between his brilliant eyes.

"What's this, eh?" He touched my brooch. "Norwegian?"

He was right, of course. Solje jewelry, characterized by tiny spoons dangling from a golden circle, is definitely Norwegian but I had my excuse ready.

"I couldn't find the Finnish brooch. I guess Mom took it with her up to the Mayo."

Naturally, my answer worked. Arvo hates for people to confuse us with other Scandinavians, but he feels terrible about Pops's accident and is protective of me. I thought my use of the popular expression "up to the Mayo" was a nice touch.

"Of course, of course. The parade was good, eh? What did you think of my beautiful Liisa?"

I studied his face. I knew he wasn't ignorant of the firestorm he'd set off in choosing his houseguest to play St. Lucy, and I was a little surprised he'd raise such a sore topic with me. Was it a challenge to his authority, or was he really just that besotted

with Liisa? "She looked lovely," I said, honestly. I considered reminding him of his faux pas but didn't have the heart to do it. Surely Ronja was over her snit by now, and it was always impossible to stay angry with him. Arvo was not only Pops's best friend; he was like an uncle to Sofi and me. For us, and even for Charlie, he'd often dressed as Santa Claus, or *Joulupukki,* on Christmas Eve and come to the house laden with gifts and asking *"Onko täällä kilttejä lapsia?"* which, translated, means, "Are there any well-behaved children here?" I smiled at him. "She looked exactly like all the pictures of St. Lucy. Is she here tonight?"

"Ei, no." His bright smile dimmed. "She has a frog in her throat. *Aiti* insisted upon putting her to bed with some Vicks."

The reference to Vicks VapoRub made me smile. Pops was fond of saying that if Vicks and a sauna can't cure you, you are on your way to the marble orchard. But I was a trifle concerned when he referred to Pauline as "mother."

"She calls you *aiti* and *isa?*"

"No, no. It is just Pauline's and my little game. It feels good, Hatti-girl, to finally be a papa."

The nip of concern deepened. Maybe Sofi was right. Maybe the Makis had gotten too involved with the lovely teenage guest.

"Don't forget that she is leaving next fall," I reminded him. "I understand she wants to study up at Marquette."

"She wants to be a professional singer," Arvo agreed, "but she could study in Hancock, too."

He was referring to Finlandia University. The only educational institution with Finnish roots in the United States was located twelve miles south of us in Hancock. I wondered if Arvo had visions of Liisa continuing to live at the funeral home and commuting to college and, if so, how Liisa felt about that.

"Finally I know how your papa feels. It is the most wonderful thing in the world to be blessed with a daughter."

The sound of footsteps on the stairs behind me caused me to excuse myself, as I didn't want to get held up chatting with one of the Burberry overcoat crowd.

"I'd better get into the kitchen to help Elli."

"Pauline is already there. *Voi kua,* Hatti," he said. "I married a worker bee."

I noted the live candles on Elli's ten-foot white pine, and the hand-knitted Nordic Christmas ornaments our circle had worked on in November that were dangling from the antlers over the fireplace, as I made my way through the parlor. I waved in the direction of Aunt Ianthe, who was plunking out "Jingle Bells" on Elli's old upright and her friend, Miss Irene Suutula, in a chair nearby awaiting her turn.

The dining room, where long buffet tables were set with red and green Christmas linens topped with evergreen centerpieces, appeared to be empty at first glance, but a slight movement near the arched window caught my eye, and I realized there was a couple standing there. They weren't speaking but I could feel the tension radiating from them as if it were a living thing. I quickly forgot them, though, when I stepped into Elli's state-of-the-art kitchen. Half a dozen women chattered as they filled bowls and trays and prepared the chafing dishes that would keep the food warm. Elli was removing something from her wall oven, but before I could report for duty, my sister had grabbed my arm and hauled me into a semi-private corner.

"Did you see what was going on in the dining room?"

"You mean the couple by the window?"

"It's Sonya. Sonya and the hunk."

"The hunk" was one of the sobriquets bestowed on our newest male resident, Max Guthrie, a transplanted cowboy who had recently purchased Namagok, the long-abandoned fishing camp that lay between Red Jacket and the Copper Eagle reservation, home of the Ojibwe nation. Max was fortyish, tall and loose-limbed, with a shock of brown hair and warm brown eyes that held a fact and a promise: He'd spent most of those forty years either with horses or women, and he knew exactly what to do with each. Privately, I thought of him as beefcake on the hoof.

"What's the big deal? They're probably just talking."

"They're not talking. That's the big deal. They're leaning. There's something going on between those two, Hatti, mark my words."

Since both Sonya and Max were single, at least as far as anyone knew, there seemed to be no potential scandal but I knew Sofi wasn't thinking about that. She was worried for me because, for some inexplicable reason, Max had shown a decided interest in me, and Sofi assumed that, underneath my "take-it-or-leave-it" attitude, I cared and could get hurt. I shrugged.

"Sonya usually avoids him. I don't think she even likes him."

"Guess, again, Sherlock. There are definite sparks flying out there."

"Hostile sparks, maybe."

"Hate's the other side of love," she pointed out, and I knew she was talking about herself. I wished, not for the first time, there was a way to fix her broken marriage.

"It doesn't matter," I reminded her, gently. "I'm still married."

Elli's voice reached me in spite of the din.

"Hatti, can you garnish the pineapple crunch cake for Diane?"

"Sure." I stepped over to the stainless-steel–topped island where Diane Hakala, wife of Red Jacket's pharmacist, was transferring cake slices onto Elli's Danish Christmas plates.

"Just put a dollop of whipped cream and a cherry on each."

Diane, middle-aged and matronly, her gray-blond hair twisted into an old-fashioned beehive, had on the unofficial dress uniform of the Keweenaw: an embroidered sweatshirt with a sewn-on collar. Silver bells dangled from her ears. "It's the coconut that makes it so moist," she explained, handing me a sample. I smacked my lips. It was delicious. An instant later, Ronja Laplander, dressed in the plain dark blue jumper and white sweater of a Sami reindeer herder, burst through the swinging door. Below her thick brow, her dark eyes flashed like the beacon in a lighthouse during a storm at sea.

"His majesty," she said, her voice dripping with sarcasm, "wants to know when supper will be served."

Arvo, it seemed, had not yet been forgiven.

"You can't blame her," Diane said, after Ronja had disappeared. "Arvo messed up big time with that St. Lucy thing."

I remembered suddenly that Diane had a teenage daughter, too.

"You don't seem upset about it. Didn't Barb want the title?"

"*Voi kahua,*" she said, which was not exactly swearing but close. "Barb was St. Lucy last year. Don't you remember?"

I felt a warmth in my cheeks. Last year at this time I had just returned home from D.C. I stayed in a cocoon of misery through Christmas and most of the month of January. Something else niggled in the back of my mind. During one of her rants, Ronja had said the pharmacist's wife was unhappy about Liisa, too. For some reason I was curious about that.

"Are Barb and Liisa friends?"

She served a few more cake slices in silence, which made me even more curious.

"Diane?"

"My daughter was friendly with her at first."

"And then?" I had no idea why I was probing. None of this was my business.

Diane shrugged her solid shoulders. "And then nothing." There was another brief silence. "She stole Barb's boyfriend."

Ah. I paused, a dollop of whipped cream dripping from my spoon. "I didn't know."

"Barb and Matti have been together since first grade. Their wedding is—was—scheduled for June. After graduation."

It was a familiar story on the Keweenaw, where high school represented the end of the educational line for most of the kids, like my sister. Teenagers jumped from homework to housekeeping to Happy Meals without passing "Go" or getting a chance to explore and learn and grow. Still, it was what they wanted.

"I'm sorry."

"She bewitched him." The vicious note in Diane's voice surprised me. "They only went on one date, and then she dumped him. Matti wasn't good enough for the princess."

"Matti?"

"Matti Murso, Tauno's boy. You know Tauno down at the Gas 'n Go."

I knew Tauno by his tattoo, "Born to Lose," which was visible on his left upper arm all summer. Just then the door that led to the back of the house opened, and Pauline Maki appeared. She wore a winter white wool sweater and a pair of neatly creased matching slacks. Her short, mousy brown hair had been professionally streaked and styled, and the perfectly applied makeup made her long, sallow face almost pretty. I admired Pauline. It couldn't have been easy to leave Detroit and come to live in a funeral home in an insular community like ours, but she was invariably cheerful and poised, and everyone knew she adored our sometime favorite son, Arvo. She was competent, too, and it was no secret that her organizational skills and work ethic were behind the execution of Arvo's endless schemes on behalf of Red Jacket.

"You smell like snow," I said. "Did you just come from outside?"

She chuckled. "One of the Lansing guests mentioned he

needed gifts to take home, so I ran over to my house to pick up some jars of thimbleberry jam."

The funeral home was only fifty yards away, located, as it was, on the other side of the Queen Anne.

"That accounts for the roses in your cheeks," I said, relieved that she appeared to have recovered from Ronja's attack of the afternoon.

"How's Liisa?" Elli asked, appearing at my elbow. I made a face. I'd already forgotten about the girl's illness.

Pauline's carefully shaped brows collided over her long, narrow nose.

"Sleeping like a baby, thank goodness. She came home from the parade with the worst sore throat and sniffles, but I made her some tea with honey and used Vicks on her chest. She should be fine for tomorrow."

"Good," Elli said. She turned to me. "When you're finished with the cake, could you serve Edna's cabbage?" My cousin knew me so well. I grinned at her.

"I was hoping you'd ask."

The guests from Lansing, along with the members of the Keweenaw Finnish-American Society, aka the members of St. Heikki's Lutheran, descended on the smorgasbord like starving wolves and made short work of the lutefisk, pasty potatoes, *pulla,* Christmas ham with prunes, *Karjalan Piirakkas*—which are Karelian Rice pies, *Joulutortut,* the Christmas tarts, and *glögi,* a mulled wine.

In no time at all we were back in the kitchen on KP, albeit without most of our workforce. Ronja, Diane and Sofi left early to chaperone the Snowflake Dance in the high-school gym, and Pauline was helping her husband entertain the out-of-town visitors. Aunt Ianthe and Miss Irene had come out to the kitchen to help.

"Are you feeling well, Henrikki?" my aunt asked, peering into my face. "You look peaked."

"Just tired," I assured her. She wiggled her nose like an inquisitive rabbit.

"*Voi kauhia!* Please don't tell me you ate some of Edna's cabbage. You know it doesn't agree with you. Irene," she said, hailing her faithful companion, "do you remember how Hatti's face swelled up that time she ate the cabbage at the church potluck?"

Twenty years earlier I'd caught the mumps the night of a church dinner, and Edna's cabbage had been blamed. The fact was, I'd never touched the cabbage, but the incident became one of those stories that refused to die, the mixed blessing-slash-curse of living in a small, insular community.

"I didn't eat any cabbage tonight." Or ever. I waited for Miss Irene's comment and was not disappointed.

" 'The rod and reproof give wisdom but the child who gets his own way brings shame to his mother, Proverbs 29:15.' "

Miss Irene's habit of finding a Bible verse for every occasion might have grown tedious, but the fact that she was always full of goodwill and that the verses were almost always off the mark, made it more amusing than anything else. Even after all these years I found myself looking forward to hearing what she'd chosen. Amazingly enough, she almost never repeated. Elli and I traded grins as the door opened to admit Arvo. Max was with him, and, in spite of what I'd told Sofi, my heart thumped a little harder.

"Ah, Elli." Arvo smacked a kiss on my cousin's cheek. "A triumph, my dear. A nearly perfect evening."

Elli thanked him.

"Why 'nearly perfect'?" I asked, mostly because my reaction to Max Guthrie annoyed me. I wasn't ready for another relationship, and I wasn't yet divorced.

Pauline Maki smiled. "One of the committeemen, Howard

Lessman, told Arvo he'd chosen the perfect Swedish girl to play St. Lucy."

I winced, imagining Arvo's dilemma. He hated having people confuse us with the Norwegians or the Danes, but, most of all, he hated having folks mistake us for Swedes. Yet he couldn't afford to offend a man who had it in his power to grant us a station on the Snow Train. It must have cost him to hold his tongue. Nearly perfect, indeed.

"Pauline and I must dash," he said. "I am anxious to check on Liisa." He waved at the rest of us. "See you all in the morning."

A few minutes later the dishes were finished, the cloths were drying on the racks, the countertops were cleared and scrubbed and ready for the morning's breakfast preparations. It was time to go. Aunt Ianthe and Miss Irene declined my offer to walk them across the street to their duplex, and Elli excused herself to check on the guests upstairs. Max and I were alone in the gleaming kitchen.

"A long day," he said.

I nodded, unaccountably tongue-tied.

"I liked the box."

"The box?"

"Your costume. The Magic Sampo?"

I laughed. "Right. Einar disapproved. He didn't think it showed my figure to advantage."

Max's deep brown eyes laughed at me. "He's forgotten the basic rule of attraction. Give a guy a hint and let him imagine the rest."

Did the light flirting mean anything? Was he testing the waters with me? Just what did he want? I couldn't ask that question, so I tried another.

"Max," I said, suddenly, "what made you come up here to the Keweenaw?"

His easy smile stayed in place, but the laughter faded from his eyes.

"I wanted a fresh start."

I could relate to that. I nodded. I wanted to ask him if there was anything between him and Sonya, but it seemed intrusive, and, really, I didn't need to know.

"Can I walk you home?"

"It's only a few yards. And you know what they say, 'there's never any crime on the Keweenaw.' "

"I wasn't thinking about crime."

I chuckled even as I reflected that his charm bordered on criminal.

I shrugged into my parka, then took his arm as we slogged through the snow. I wondered if he expected me to invite him in and whether that was what I wanted. Before I could figure it out we'd reached the front porch, and I heard the tinny notes of my ringtone, something by Rihanna, chosen by Charlie. I sighed and dug the phone out of my pocket. "A police chief's work is never done," I said. I held the phone to my ear. "This is Hatti."

"Hatti." I had never heard such anguish expressed in the two syllables of any word, much less my name. Fear knifed through me.

"Pauline? What is it?" Then I remembered she was the funeral director's wife, and my fear increased. "Has something happened to my parents?"

"No, no, it's not that. Oh, Hatti." A sob cut off her words, and I gazed helplessly at Max.

"What is it?"

"You have to come over, now."

"Max Guthrie is here," I said, half hoping she'd give me permission to bring him. "Could he help?"

"No, oh, no. Just you. Come now." Her voice seemed to fade like a flashlight whose battery had run down.

"I'll be right there." I started to hang up, but she spoke again, and there was unmistakable pain behind the cry.

"Oh, Hatti, she's dead, she's dead!"

I felt a coldness behind my nose and a heavy weight in my stomach. I had to force the question out of my mouth.

"Who's dead?"

"St. Lucy."

I blinked. "St. Lucy? You mean Liisa?"

"She's dead," Pauline sobbed. "Murdered. Hatti, someone murdered her!"

CHAPTER THREE

Most of the houses on the Keweenaw are modest, wooden, two-story affairs more than fifty years old with steeply pitched rooflines to limit snow accumulation and the windows set as high as possible to prevent snow drifts from blocking the light.

During the heyday of the copper mines, though, the wealthy mine managers built mansions for their large families. My parents' Queen Anne Victorian and Elli's inn were both designed by noted architects of the late nineteenth century. The third house on our block, the one belonging to Arvo and Pauline Maki, also had been fashioned for a well-to-do family, but its architect must have had a premonition of what the future held for the structure. I found it impossible to imagine a house with a gloomier aspect.

The Maki Funeral Home was characterized by large, dark stones and narrow windows that reminded me of arrow slits in a Norman castle. The heavy, thick, shingled roof curled over the gutters and drainpipes like a python closing in on its supper. Dense evergreens bordered the stone walkway, and, as I approached the black double doors, I felt a familiar atavistic tremor in my stomach. I'd experienced that sensation every time I'd ever entered the Makis' home, undoubtedly because I associated it with death.

"And, apparently," I muttered, "nothing has changed."

Tonight the plain evergreen wreaths on the doors conveyed the message that those within were observing the holiday, but in a quiet way so as not to offend any mourners. Sucked into the depressing atmosphere of the place, I couldn't immediately lift my fist to knock, and I searched for my *sisu*, that indomitable persistence that we, here on the Keweenaw, prize so highly. Before I could find it, Pauline Maki opened the door. Her face was drawn and pale as it had been that morning after the altercation with Ronja. Normally the soul of courtesy and practical consideration, she neither greeted me nor asked me to remove my boots. She gave a little sob, turned toward the corridor that led to the ground-floor kitchen and began to walk away from me. I followed her like Alice after the White Rabbit.

The doors on the right that belonged to Arvo's office and the embalming room were closed. The double doors on the left were open, and I glanced into the dark recesses of the chapel as we passed it. I felt disoriented and untethered as we plunged into the bowels of the spooky house, and I concentrated on keeping Pauline in sight as we made our way through the cold, darkened downstairs kitchen, out the back door and into the greenhouse that connected the house and the sauna. The natural light from the glass-paneled roof, along with the scents of soil and peat and plants, created a slight uptick in my spirits, but we soon left it behind. As we were standing in front of the sauna door, Pauline finally spoke.

"I hate this place," she muttered. I'd never heard venom in her voice. I'd never even heard displeasure. I stared at her. "I've always hated it."

There was no time to think about her words because she turned the handle and opened the door. I inhaled the familiar and comforting scent of cedar. In our community, sauna is more than a bath. It is more than relaxation, too. It is a place for socializing and even ritual. Finns and Finnish-Americans sauna at least weekly. It was one of the things I'd missed most during my six months in D.C.

My sense of wellbeing was short-lived. Pauline stepped aside, giving me an excellent view of the body on the wooden floor. My stomach roiled and lurched. I could see that Liisa's sky-blue eyes were open even though she was lying on her stomach with one hand tucked under her breastbone and the other arm outflung. Her feet, small, bare and well-shaped, stuck out of the end of her white robe. I noticed a dark, ugly blob of coagulated blood near one shell-colored ear. Her cheek had lost its porcelain glow. Now it just looked pale and clammy and dead. After a moment, I realized there was another living person in the room. He was seated on the *lavat*, or low bench, and he was bent double, his forehead nearly on his knees, his arms wrapped around his waist in a futile attempt to find comfort. I felt desperately sorry for him and for Pauline, but I felt worse for Liisa Pelonen, who would not become a professional singer or even finish high school. Anger surged through me, and I grabbed onto the door frame to steady myself at the same time that Pauline moved next to her husband. She squeezed his shoulder, and he began to sob.

I waited until the worst of it was over before I spoke.

"What happened," I asked, finally. "An accident?" I remembered, belatedly, that Pauline had called it murder.

"*Joo.*" Arvo's affirmative was muffled.

"No," said his wife, at the same time. "Not an accident." Pauline's voice didn't tremble. She had obviously recovered from the first shock and had begun to analyze the situation in her practical way. "Look at her temple, Hatti. Someone hit her with a rock."

"She fell on the rock, Pauly," Arvo said, wearily. "No one hit her."

I knelt next to the girl and tried to smooth a few wheat-colored tendrils away from her wound, but they were stuck in the blood. The gash looked fairly deep to me. My eyes strayed to the sauna rock lying a foot away from her nose. I'd seen lots of sauna rocks in my life but almost never out of the stove. I'd never known one to fall out accidentally. I thought it extremely unlikely that a rock had rolled out of the wood-burning heater and caused Liisa to stumble over it. Even if she had slipped on the rock, I didn't think she'd have landed that close to it.

"How did the rock get out of the stove?" I said, thinking aloud. "And why would she have tripped on it? The light goes on as soon as you open the door."

"She may have fainted," Arvo said.

"Unlikely." I was offering questions and answers by instinct. "She was a Finlander. She'd have known how long she could stay in the bath. And, anyway, she's fully clothed." And that brought up another question. "Why would she sauna in her clothes? Her costume?"

"Why would anyone hit our girl? Everyone loved her."

I thought about Ronja Laplander and Diane Hakala and how he was, as usual, ascribing his own feelings to everyone else.

I stared at the wound. Something about it wasn't right. Shouldn't there be more blood?

"This wasn't an accident," Pauline said, an edge of steel in her voice. "Someone broke into the sauna and hit her in the head with that stone. Whoever it was probably cleaned up the blood."

I wondered what possible reason someone could have for smashing in Liisa Pelonen's skull, then tidying up afterwards, but I said nothing. It wasn't really my business.

"Not only that," Pauline said, warming to her theory, "I put that girl to bed in her rosebud nightgown. This fiend must have forced her to get out of bed, to put on the St. Lucy costume and to come down here to the sauna so that it would take us a long time to find her. This was no random murder. It was a heinous plot." Her voice had gotten louder and more wobbly, and suddenly she broke, dissolving in a torrent of tears.

His wife's distress finally shook Arvo out of his cocoon of sorrow. He lumbered to his feet, ungainly as a hibernating bear returning to the land of the conscious. He put his arm around Pauline's slim shoulders, and she rested her head against his chest.

"We should call the sheriff," I reminded them, gently.

"*Ei.* No," Arvo said. "I am not turning my girl over to that horse's ass."

I was shocked. I'd never heard Arvo speak so crudely.

"No Clump," he repeated. "I can't bear to see him take her away in the meat wagon. You must handle this, Hatti. You will handle it. You are police chief."

"You know I'm not qualified to handle the investigation of a suspicious death," I said gently. "I have no access to forensic equipment, and if I had, I wouldn't know what to do with it. We have to notify her father, and we have to call the sheriff."

"If you won't do this, I will do it myself," Arvo said, his voice cracking. "Of course we must find justice for our *tytto* but no Clump. Not yet."

"Hatti has a point, dear," Pauline said, with her usual good sense. "She isn't a trained police officer." She gazed at me, a pleading look in her hazel eyes. "On the other hand, you went to law school."

"For one year. I only got as far as torts."

"And you worked for a lawyer."

"I didn't work for him; I was married to him." Pauline ignored my interjections.

"And you are a writer, which means you are curious."

I thought fleetingly of my half-forgotten dream of writing novels.

"I write a knitting blog and run a bait shop, neither of which qualifies me to investigate a murder."

Pauline switched her argument from my obvious lack of qualifications to appeal to my sense of community responsibility.

"And then there's the festival. This will ruin *Pikkujoulu*. We will not get the Snow Train designation, and all will have been in vain." Arvo dropped his head into his hands and groaned.

"That would be a shame, of course, but if Liisa was murdered, we have a duty to report it," I pointed out virtuously.

"And then there's the police department and Carl's job," she continued. "If Sheriff Clump takes over, he will surely use this as a wedge to get the law enforcement contract."

I had no doubt that was true, and I felt my resistance crumbling.

"That's enough," Arvo said, gently. "If Hatti does not want to do this, we shouldn't pressure her." His heavy sigh broke my heart. "We can call the state police."

Pauline wasn't ready to give up.

"What about the festival?"

Arvo sighed, looking up at her. "What does it matter?"

The hopelessness in his voice was so unlike Arvo. I just couldn't bear adding to his grief and distress.

"What about this," I said, thinking as I spoke. Or, rather, not thinking. "It's Friday night. I will spend the next two days trying to find an explanation for this. If I can't find one by Sunday night, we will contact the sheriff, or possibly the state police."

Pauline's tight face relaxed, and Arvo came over to put his arm around my shoulders.

"Thank you, Hatti-girl," he said, using Pops's nickname for me. "It's what she would have wanted." he said. He gazed at the body on the floor, and his voice trembled. "Liisa loved Red Jacket, she loved *Pikkujoulu* and she loved being in the pageant." His face twisted. "*Voi kauhia!* Who will play St. Lucy?"

I pictured Ronja Laplander's furious countenance. At least

someone would benefit from this shockingly tragic turn of events.

"I imagine Astrid Laplander knows the part," I murmured. "You could give her a call."

"All right then," Arvo said. "That is settled. You should go home and get a good night's sleep," he told me.

"Okay."

"Wait," Pauline said. "You need to take statements from us. We're the ones who found the body."

I made a face. *Of course.* Investigation Techniques 101: Interview whomever found the body.

"Right."

"I'll get you a notebook." Pauline was never at a loss. It occurred to me that *she* should be investigating this suspicious death. "Tomorrow I will tell everyone that Liisa is in bed with a fever."

Arvo flinched, but he patted his wife's arm.

"I do not know what I would do without you, dear, eh? You think of everything."

CHAPTER FOUR

My mind was spinning when I let myself into the house a short time later. What had I agreed to do? Break the law, probably. It had to be some kind of a crime not to report a suspicious death to the cops. I found myself trying to remember all the *Murder, She Wrotes,* and the *NCISes* and *Midsomer Murders* I'd seen. Years earlier I'd been a big fan of Agatha Christie, Dorothy L. Sayers and all the rest of the mystery writers. Had those detectives used any special techniques? Observation, of course, and intuition. And, of course, those private eyes had an undeniable advantage: Someone (the writer) was orchestrating their lives.

Well, I didn't have a writer, and my intuition had failed me in the biggest decision of my life. I'd have to rely on logic derived from organization, a dubious prospect considering I'm the queen of clutter. I shook off the worries. I'd make a spreadsheet listing potential suspects, motives and so forth, but, at the moment, I could think of only one person who wanted Liisa Pelonen out of the way this weekend, and it seemed inconceivable that Ronja Laplander, a mother of five, would attack a teenage girl with a rock.

Almost inconceivable. It occurred to me that this would be a particularly difficult task since I knew virtually everyone in Red Jacket and couldn't imagine a murderer among them. Could the killer be an outsider? Could someone have come to the parade yesterday, have seen Liisa and, for whatever reason, decided to kill her? That seemed unlikely. Whoever it was would have had to know that she lived with the Makis, that she was home alone. Why, I wondered, not for the first time, was she rigged out as St. Lucy? There was no scenario I could think of that would account for that.

I took off my jacket. Larry had waddled out to the foyer, so I bent down to rub his ears.

"I just agreed to investigate what looks like a murder," I told him, "then I promptly left the body on the floor of the sauna and came home to get a good night's rest. Not a brilliant start. I probably should have found a camera and taken pictures, then made a taped outline, because you know as well as I do that Arvo isn't going to leave that girl on the floor." Larry was considerate enough to say nothing, allowing me to think. "There should be an autopsy, but that can't happen until we officially report Liisa's death." I thought for another minute. Somewhat to my amazement, I came up with a brilliant plan.

"Sonya," I told Larry. "Sonya's the answer."

I retrieved my phone and punched in my friend's number. She didn't answer, which either meant the power had died on her phone, or she was out in the back of beyond delivering a baby and had lost cell service. I left a message that I needed to speak with her in the morning.

It occurred to me suddenly that someone needed to talk to Jalmer Pelonen. I called the funeral home number and waited through eight rings. Arvo's voice sounded so subdued that I guessed he and Pauline had been crying again.

"Someone needs to tell Jalmer Pelonen," I said.

"He's ice fishing at Gogebic," Arvo said. "He always goes the first two weeks in December. He should be home tomorrow, and I will take care of it."

After I hung up, I wondered if I should go to see Jalmer myself but decided that Liisa's real father would take the news better from another man. Jalmer Pelonen lived in a cabin near

Ahmeek. He was known to be a hermit. I couldn't remember ever seeing him on the streets of Red Jacket, and he certainly wouldn't know me. I wondered where he got his supplies. I wondered what it had been like for Liisa, growing up with only her father for company. No wonder she had turned to music. Had she enjoyed living with the Makis, only blocks away from her new high school? They were questions I'd need to ask.

I found a fresh pad of paper and a pencil, settled into Pops's oversized leather chair in the study that still smelled like cherry tobacco, some five years after my mother had made him stop smoking his pipe. Lined with books, anchored by a big, oak desk and lighted with paned windows, this was my favorite room in the house. First, I told myself, I'd make a list of suspects and their motives and then I'd create a spreadsheet on the computer. I wrote down Ronja's name and stared at it. Inconceivable.

A half hour later there was still just the one name on my pad, and I was being nudged awake by Larry's wet nose in my hand. It was time to let him out and go to bed. The catnap had served one purpose, I told myself. I'd awakened with a brilliant idea. I had survived the breakup of my marriage with the help of my friends. Didn't it make sense to tackle this project with what I knew was a winning strategy? In the morning, I decided, I'd talk to Sonya, then I'd talk to Sofi and Elli. If the Keweenawesome Knitters (the name we'd decided on for our knitting circle) couldn't figure out what happened to Liisa Pelonen, I'd eat my hat. Or turn this over to Sheriff Clump. And, frankly, neither of those options appealed to me.

Just before I went to sleep for a second time that night I realized what had happened. Or, rather, what had not happened. I'd stared at a dead girl and taken on a heavy responsibility for which I was totally unprepared, and I had not experienced a galloping heartbeat. I had not fainted. I had not even feared that I would faint. I had had no hot flashes or nausea. I had not screamed.

There had been no panic attack.

"Thank you, God," I whispered. Miss Irene would have said it more eloquently but with no more sincerity than I felt at that moment. "Thank you, God."

The relentlessly cheery voice jerked me awake.

"Roll up your sleeves," chirped Betty Ann Pritula, the Keweenaw's answer to Martha Stewart, "and roll out your dough! Today we're going to make old-fashioned gingerbread houses!"

Betty Ann's radio program, *The Finnish Line,* or, as Pops calls it "Let Me Finnish You Off," is listened to seven days a week the length and breadth of the Keweenaw. She dispenses information, like the weather and recipes, but her forte is telling people what to do and where to go. She could have given Napoleon a run for his money.

While I pulled on a pair of bright red corduroy jeans and a light green sweatshirt emblazoned with the words: LONDON, PARIS, NEW YORK, ISHPEMING, I listened to Betty Ann's tribute to her own recipe for royal icing, a product that was so sticky and so reliable that if it had been used at the battle of Jericho, she claimed, those walls would never have come tumbling down.

"Royal icing," she maintained, as if her listeners were marshaling their arguments against her, "has stood the test of time. Like Vicks."

I froze, my fingers locked around the handle of my hairbrush. Pauline had used Vicks VapoRub on Liisa last night during the girl's last hour of life. A heavy sadness tugged at my heart. She'd been so young. And so beautiful. I knew that's what everyone would say when the truth was finally out. It was such a shame she died. She was so young and so beautiful, as if the less beautiful among us were expendable. Betty Ann's voice intruded again.

"And be sure you stop by the first annual Finnish Christmas Pageant in Red Jacket today. It is called *Pikkujoulu*, or 'Little Christmas.' For those of you not in the know, 'Little Christmas' refers to the parties we hold in our homes during the early weeks of December. Finnish arts and crafts will be sold, as well as refreshments from Main Street Floral and Fudge and Patty's Pasties in the merchants' booths under the brand-new tarpaulin in the Copper County High School parking lot. That's on the corner of Main and Third. You can't miss it."

I knew she was reading Arvo's press release word for word, and I had to admit it sounded pretty good.

"Entertainment will be provided by the Muskrat Marching Band, and at two o'clock you can stroll down the road to St. Heikki's Finnish Lutheran, where you will be entertained with a traditional St. Lucy's Day pageant, this year starring Miss Liisa Pelonen in the title role."

I snapped off the radio feeling slightly sick.

A short time later I made a pot of coffee while Larry wended his way through the backyard snow maze I'd created especially for him. When he came back in I picked the snow crystals out of the spaces between his toes, something Pops had taught me to do long ago. No one, he'd said, liked to have cold feet. Not even dogs. I poured a cup of coffee and grabbed my cell and headed for the study.

It was six-thirty, a smidgeon too early to call anybody, so I sipped my coffee, wished Red Jacket still had a daily newspaper and gazed out the arched window at the falling snow. I had between zero and one suspects because I couldn't really believe Ronja Laplander had had anything to do with Liisa Pelonen's death. I'd have to start from scratch. I'd have to find out everything I could about Liisa, about her family and her friends. I'd draw up a profile of the dead girl, and, in doing that, names would emerge. Names, I hoped, of possible suspects.

I closed my eyes and tried to remember the main motives for murder and came up with three. Greed, of course; revenge and jealousy. The first one was out. Liisa had been a high school senior who had transferred to Copper County High after her small high school had closed. She'd moved in with the Makis because her father, who lived out near Ahmeek, couldn't afford to buy her a car. No, it couldn't be greed.

What about revenge? Would Ronja have killed Liisa because she was angry at Arvo? It seemed unlikely. No, my best shot was jealousy. Liisa had been a talented singer, as beautiful as a slender, blonde eighteen-year-old could be and, big surprise, not liked by the girls at school. And yet, Arvo and Pauline had loved her like a daughter. The whole thing was clearly a mystery, and I fought a jolt of panic at the thought that it was up to me to unravel it.

The ring tone sounded distressingly loud in the quiet of the winter morning. My heart jerked against my ribs as I answered the phone.

Someone laughed. "It sounds like I woke you."

I pressed my palm against my chest. It was only Sonya. "I was just startled. How are you?"

"Good. On my way over to Frog Creek. Mrs. Kaukola's ready to deliver her seventh, and, as she's told me every single time I've seen her, she doesn't hold with hospitals. I'm just praying she won't want to give birth in the sauna."

"I wouldn't hold my breath. Giving birth in the sauna is a time-honored tradition both in Finland and here. At one time it was the warmest and most sanitary place around."

"So I've heard. So what's up?"

"Brace yourself for a shock. Liisa Pelonen's dead. Arvo and

Pauline found her last night. She was in their sauna, and, from the wound on her head, I'd guess she was battered by a sauna rock." I heard her quick intake of breath and a murmur of distress. "They asked me to investigate on the Q.T., at least until after the festival. The thing is, I need your help."

"You want me to take a look at the body?"

One of the things I loved about Sonya was her quick grasp of things. Another thing I loved was her acceptance about my role in this. I knew Elli would start calling me "Sherlock," and Sofi would roll her eyes when she heard about it. But they'd help me. The Keweenawesome Knitters were like the four musketeers.

"That's exactly it. Do you mind?"

"I'll do it as soon as I get number seven delivered."

"I really appreciate this." I did, too. I also appreciated that she didn't point out that she wasn't an official coroner, that she didn't have access to a lab and that it was probably a crime to fail to report this to the proper authorities. "The Makis may be at the festival."

"Key in the milk chute?"

I grinned. Since nearly all our homes had been built while there was still home milk delivery, everyone had a milk chute, and since we all feared freezing to death more than random break-ins, we'd developed the habit of leaving a spare key in the now useless cubbies. I was impressed that Sonya, who'd lived here less than two years, had taken the trouble to learn our customs.

"Yup."

"Hatti? Do you think Liisa was murdered?"

"I'm hoping you can tell me."

There was a short silence. "If you need any professional help with the investigation," she said, hesitantly, "you might talk with Max Guthrie. I understand he was some kind of a cop in his previous life."

The suggestion revealed that Sonya knew just how far out of my depth I was. It also revealed that she knew more about Max than the rest of us.

"Thanks," I said. "I might just do that."

My mother's mantel clock chimed. It was time to head over to the inn for the breakfast smorgasbord being held for the benefit of the out-of-town guests.

The first person I saw, when I stepped into Elli's kitchen, was Pauline Maki, pulling a dish of baked eggs out of the oven. This morning she wore a crisp black and cream striped sweater with black wool slacks. She'd applied her makeup, as always, but I could see the pallor underneath and the resulting effect was somewhat ghoulish. There were purple circles under her eyes, too. I imagined that neither she nor Arvo had slept much last night and felt guilty about my own restful night.

"Hey, Hatti," Elli said, her eyes bright. She wore a hand-knitted red sweater with a yoke of white snowflakes, and she was carrying an oversized tray filled with Finnish pastries. "Liisa's got a fever of a hundred and two; can you believe it? She won't be able to play St. Lucy this afternoon. Poor kid."

"That's a shame," I said, wondering when I could talk to Elli about the business. Probably not now. She had enough on her plate. Literally.

"The child's very disappointed," Pauline murmured. "She tried to get up, but that just made her dizzy. We had to insist that she stay in bed." The lie was facile and smooth, and I knew I shouldn't be surprised. Pauline had had all night to work on it.

"Please tell her how sorry I am," Elli said. "She did such a lovely job yesterday."

"I will."

I realized I'd need to talk with Pauline again, but we heard

45

voices and laughter in the dining room and knew it was time to serve the meal.

While I was positioning the tray of *kylmagavustettu lohi,* a traditional salmon dish, a string bean of a girl bounded up and grabbed me from the back.

"Morning, Aunt Hatti," she yodeled.

I put down the spatula and hugged her back. At fifteen, Charlie's an excellent student when she wants to be and a technical wizard. She's inherited the dark hair and green eyes of her father, not the blond, blue-eyed coloring that so many of the rest of us have, and she wears round Harry Potter glasses that make her look like an inquisitive baby owl.

"Good morning, my favorite niece."

"I'm your only niece." Charlie was a very literal young lady. "Can I have one of those blinis?"

I nodded and watched her swipe the food from a nearby tray.

"How's the cop business," she asked, eyeing me strangely. "Arrested anybody yet?"

I tried to laugh, but I'm not great at subterfuge, and Charlie's smart. Real smart. She peered through her lenses.

"Okay, Aunt Hatti. What's going on?"

My great aunt Ianthe has always maintained that Charlie and I, like herself, have the Finnish second-sight. I knew she was wrong about me, but I wasn't sure about Charlie. The girl was always five steps ahead of everybody else except on the occasions when she behaved like a child.

"What kind of a question is that, Snork Maiden?"

I tried to put her off by using her old childhood nickname, a character from *The Moomins,* a series of children's stories featuring a family of hippos.

The ploy was unsuccessful.

"You're so transparent, Aunt Hatti," she said. "You'd better never try to get a job with the CIA."

"I won't," I promised. I had no intention of going back to Washington, D.C. Not ever.

"So, tell me."

Elli bustled up to us with a tray of omelets. "Pauline's really taking this Liisa thing hard," she murmured. "She looks like death warmed over."

"She's probably just tired," I said, aware of Charlie studying my all-too-revealing face. Sofi's voice, unusually harsh, cut off our conversation.

"Charlotte Teljo! I could use some help with these muffins!"

Charlie's pleasant face twisted into an ugly scowl.

"Hey," I said, softly, "everything okay between you and your mom?"

"We're in a fight. I want to spend Christmas with my dad, and she says no."

I watched Charlie cross the room, her lower lip puckered, her feet dragging, and I wished, not for the first time, that Sofi could find a way to reconcile with her husband. Charlie needed Lars. So did Sofi, whether she'd admit it or not.

CHAPTER FIVE

The decision to hold *Pikkujoulu* in the sprawling parking lot of the high school rather than the small gymnasium had been an easy one for the Red Jacket Chamber of Commerce, but that made a large tarpaulin a necessity. After all, it was December on the Keweenaw. The snag was the cost of the tarp, which would have wiped out the chamber's entire budget for the next two years. Accordingly, no one objected when Arvo insisted upon buying it himself and donating it to the town.

It had all been easy sailing until it was time to decide on the color and lettering of said tarp. Most of us favored a neutral color, gray or brown, imprinted with something neutral like, *Red Jacket, Michigan*.

Arvo, of course, wanted something Christmas-y and bold, say a green-and-white striped canvas imprinted with bright red letters and the words: *Welcome to Pikkujoulu, the Keweenaw Peninsula's First Annual Christmas Pageant!*

In the end, we'd left the decision to the man who was footing the bill, and I'd forgotten all about the controversy until I viewed the new tarp in all its glory spread over the parking lot. I realized immediately that Pauline Maki must have ordered the somber gray canvas with the discreet black lettering that read: *Maki Funeral Parlor, Red Jacket, Michigan*.

Inside the tent, strategically placed space heaters cut the chill of the winter morning. I strolled through the honeycomb of booths. Patty Huhtasaari, owner and proprietor of *Patty's Past-*

ies, was selling her signature product along with the jellies and jams put up by an order of monks who lived and worked up in the cliffs near Eagle Harbor. A jar of thimbleberry jam caught my eye, and I shivered, remembering that Pauline had just gone home to collect several such jars and to check on Liisa the last time anyone had seen the girl alive. Anyone, that is, except the murderer.

My prime (and only) suspect, Ronja Laplander, was absent from the Copper Kettle's booth. Her husband, Armas, assisted by his younger daughters, was setting out the kitchen utensils, copper chunk magnets, woodcut ornaments of the Upper Peninsula and some of the other items available in their store. I flashed a bright smile at the stoic Finn.

"No Ronja today?"

Armas shook his head.

"Mama's at the church," said one of the younger girls, excitement and wonder in her voice. "Astrid gets to be St. Lucy, and she has to practice!"

"Lucky for Astrid," I said.

The child nodded. "Mama said it was a miracle."

A miracle created by a maniac, I thought. Was that maniac Ronja herself?

Diane Hakala, dressed in a pink, lace-trimmed sweatshirt and stretchy brown slacks that reminded me of an ice cream cone, represented Hakala's Pharmacy. At the moment she was laying out the scented sachets she created annually after drying flowers in a room at the back of her house.

"Did you hear about Liisa Pelonen?" she called out. "She's got laryngitis or something, and she's had to withdraw from the pageant this afternoon, so Astrid's getting her chance after all." I paused and studied the pleasant face under the beehive hairdo. Was there an expression of guilt there? "It almost seems like divine intervention, doesn't it?"

Her comment hit me wrong. Even if Liisa had just been home in bed with a sore throat, I couldn't believe everyone thought it was such a heaven-sent blessing.

"I doubt that God had anything to do with Liisa's absence," I said irritably.

"But it makes everything right," Diane argued. "Arvo and Pauline should never have ignored tradition."

"Pauline didn't have anything to do with it," I said, feeling a sudden, unaccountable need to defend the woman. The Makis, as the town's biggest—and only—benefactors, frequently put people's backs up, but everyone was quick to forgive our native son. I was beginning to suspect that resentment of Pauline lingered longer.

"Anyway," Barb said, knowingly, "the sore throat is Pauline's fault. Liisa was late for the practice, and when she finally showed up she wasn't even wearing long underwear. Everyone on the Keweenaw knows enough to make Halloween costumes big enough to fit over snowsuits. St. Lucy is always cold, even in long underwear!"

One word caught my attention.

"Liisa was late for the parade?"

"Nearly an hour late. Everyone was frantic. She finally sauntered in as cool as you please with no explanation given."

I made a mental note to make a timeline of Liisa's activities on the day of her death. I eyed the pharmacist's wife speculatively. This was probably a good time to get an alibi for Barb and her jilted daughter.

"How was the dance last night?"

"There weren't enough boys. The girls had to dance with each other."

My ears pricked up. "What about Matti Murso? Did he come?"

She shook her head. "He probably heard Liisa was sick," she

said, in a low, bitter voice, "and decided not to bother."

Or, maybe he decided to spend the night bashing her head in with a sauna rock.

"I thought you'd said Liisa wasn't really interested in Matti." Too late I realized I'd used the past tense, but Diane didn't seem to notice, and she automatically corrected it.

"She isn't. But he still follows her around like a little lamb. You know men. They're all slaves to their hormones."

I thought of Diane's husband, tall and distinguished with white hair, wire-rimmed glasses and a dignified, professional demeanor. If Arnold Hakala was a slave to his desires, I'd never seen any sign of it.

"Young males," Diane clarified, as if she could read my thoughts. Her next words jolted me like a triple espresso, so completely did they sum up the situation. "If only Arvo and Pauline had never offered that girl a place to live."

The Bait & Stitch booth looked warm and festive. Skeins of brightly colored yarn were piled on the table tops, and hand-knitted sweaters, shawls and baby blankets were pinned on the back panels in the booth. Great-aunt Ianthe was hanging pairs of double-strand Nordic mittens on a willow branch while Miss Irene, wedged into a lawn chair, worked on a fluffy baby sweater in Crystal Palace's peppermint pink, her hands low in her lap as she employed the continental style of knitting. Einar was perched on his favorite stool, tying flies.

I greeted them all and told them about Sonya and the Kaukola baby.

Great-aunt Ianthe clapped her hands.

"That's wonderful news! Another dear little soul enters the world."

Miss Irene beamed and quoted a surprisingly relevant verse.

" 'For you formed my inward parts; you knitted me together in my mother's womb. Psalm 139.' "

Ianthe Ollila and Irene Suutula had been born within a few months of each other and had been friends all their lives. They were a little like a Finnish Mutt and Jeff, with Ianthe taller by half a foot and a good deal heavier, but each wore her snow-white curls in a short style and each sported a pair of friendly blue eyes. As children, they'd shared a love of piano lessons, and both had attended Finlandia University. But where Miss Irene returned to Red Jacket to teach piano lessons, Aunt Ianthe taught third grade at Red Jacket Elementary School.

As far as I knew, the friendship had been threatened only once, some thirty years earlier, when the organist at St. Heikki's died. Both my aunt and her friend were interested in the position. I'd always thought it was a testament to the pastor at the time, who had used the wisdom of King Solomon to strike a compromise that had passed the test of time. Aunt Ianthe (who was not a fan of sharps or flats) was to play all hymns written in the key of "C," while Miss Irene performed everything else up to and including that jewel-in-the-crown, Sibelius's masterwork, *Olla Hiljentaa minun Henki.*

"Thank you all for running things here this morning," I said. "It looks wonderful, and it's important to me, as temporary, acting police chief, to be able to keep an eye on everything and not be tied down with a booth."

" 'Cease not to give thanks for you, making mention of you in my prayers, Ephesians 1:16.' "

"Your dear parents will be home next Thursday, I understand," Ianthe said. "I imagine you will be glad to relinquish the duties of police chief."

"Absolutely," I agreed. "Pops is welcome to this job."

"Oh, I almost forgot to show you what Irene and I found up in the attic." Aunt Ianthe held up a doll, probably eighteen inches high, with bright blue eyes and thick blond braids. She was wearing the plain white shift, red sash and the crown of candles of St. Lucy, and she looked so much like Liisa Pelonen had yesterday afternoon on Ollie's sleigh that, for a moment, I couldn't breathe.

"I made the clothes for her years ago," Ianthe continued. "Isn't she perfect for the festival?"

"Perfect." My voice came out in a squeak.

" 'There is no fear in love but perfect love casts out fear,' " Miss Irene said. " 'First John 4:18.' "

"It's a shame about dear little Liisa." Mostly, Aunt Ianthe refrained from commenting on the Biblical references. She heaved a sigh, and I wondered, just for an instant, whether she knew how much of a shame it was. I was getting paranoid. "Irene and I were so looking forward to hearing her sing at the pageant. She was late for the practice, you know, and only arrived at the church in time for the parade."

It was the second time Liisa's tardiness had been mentioned. I tried to keep my tone casual. "Why was that?"

"I expect she was with her friends," Ianthe said. "That's what Pauline said, in any case."

"Huh. She was with her friends," I repeated, hoping my aunt would expand on the explanation.

"Probably a boyfriend," Ianthe said, helpfully. "Liisa is lovely, a pretty girl." Her kind face clouded. "Pauline got a look on her face like she'd been eating lemons. She's a stickler for clockwork, that one."

" 'A time to love, a time to hate, a time for war, a time for peace,' " chirped Miss Irene. " 'Ecclesiastes 3:18.' "

"Pauline doesn't realize you have to allow young people to have their secrets," Ianthe said. "Of course, she's never been a mother."

I smiled at my aunt. She'd never been a mother, either, but she and Miss Irene had always welcomed Sofi, Elli and me into their home. They'd taught us piano and how to knit and how to make snow ice cream.

" 'For God will bring every deed into judgment, with every secret thing, whether good or evil. Ecclesiastes 12:14.' "

"Too much Ecclesiastes, Irene," Aunt Ianthe said, pleasantly. "You don't want to get into a rut, dear."

I was silent, wishing I had access to Liisa's secrets. Did her tardiness yesterday have anything to do with her grisly death some eight hours later?

A pair of trim, middle-aged women, lift tags hanging from the zippers of their expensive ski jackets, stepped into our booth.

"What an exquisite sweater," said one of them, gazing at the reindeer prancing across my aunt's generous chest. "I had no idea there was such a strong Norwegian influence in the U.P. Are the mittens for sale?"

There was a brief silence, and I knew Aunt Ianthe was trying to decide whether or not to point out that we were Finns not Norwegians, and Miss Irene was working on a suitable Bible verse. It seemed like an excellent time for me to move on, and I excused myself, stepping out into the main concourse. An instant later I felt a gentle hand at my elbow. I looked down into Miss Irene's concerned face.

"It isn't a sore throat, is it?" The hairs stood up on the back of my neck. What did the piano teacher know?

"Pauline says she has a high fever."

"She didn't look well yesterday. She looked worried."

I relaxed a little. "Maybe she was already getting sick."

"Maybe. Her eyes were shiny and glittering, but she was so pale." She paused. " 'And I looked, and behold a pale horse: and his name that sat on him was Death. Revelation 6:8.' "

I felt a cold hand wrap around my heart.

This time Miss Irene had nailed it.

I excused myself, again, and hurried down to the most popular booth at the festival where Charlie and her friend Maija

Luisa were boxing up Sofi's homemade fudge and selling it to the hungry shoppers.

After her divorce, Sofi had opened Main Street Floral and Fudge, combining her two lifelong interests. With our small population, hybrid stores are not uncommon. Fudge sales are seasonal, and flower sales are intermittent, depending as they do on weddings and funerals. The combination afforded Sofi a decent living. It also kept my sister busy, and as long as she was busy, she didn't have to think too hard about what she'd lost.

I signaled to her and to Charlie. As soon as they could get away, she joined me at an empty table in the refreshment area with cups of fresh coffee.

"What's up?" Sofi asked.

I searched her face for a moment. I didn't waste time with preliminaries.

"Arvo and Pauline found Liisa in their sauna when they got home from the smorgasbord last night. She was dead."

Sofi gasped, her brows slamming together. Her first horrified response was quickly followed by her protective instinct. "Charlie," she said, "you'd better get back to the booth."

My intrepid niece didn't even hear her mother. "I knew something terrible had happened to Liisa."

"How did you know it?" I asked, really curious.

"I don't know. It just made sense. Astrid's playing St. Lucy because Liisa's too sick. No one is ever too sick to play St. Lucy. And then there's Mrs. Maki. She looks like someone shot her dog." Charlie made a face. "Or, rather, burned down her greenhouse. And then there's you, Aunt Hatti. You look like you've got a secret."

Sofi shook her head, amused by her daughter's perspicacity, in spite of herself.

"It's her face. She never could play poker."

I ignored that and addressed myself to Charlie. "You're not

shocked to hear that a teenage girl was murdered?"

Charlie seemed to think about that.

"I think it's because it was Liisa. I mean, she's the kind of girl who would get herself murdered."

"Charlie!" Sofi's voice was too sharp and caused heads to turn. I smiled and waved at people nearby.

"No one's supposed to know," I said, out of the side of my mouth. "Not yet. I've agreed to investigate it for the next couple of days. Sonya's going to take a look at the body, and I need your help, too."

"Mine?"

I nodded. "I'd like to know everything you can tell me about Liisa." I turned to my sister. "And, I need you to put your ear to the ground. See if you can pick up any information about her."

She looked doubtful. "I'd like to go on record as saying you shouldn't have anything to do with this, Hatti."

I felt a little spear of sadness. Once upon a time, Sofi had been the intrepid one, unafraid of anything, but that was before the crumbling of her marriage.

"I didn't want to, either, at first, but Arvo and Pauline convinced me that it would be disastrous to make this public during the festival when the Snow Train station is hanging in the balance and because they didn't want to turn her"—I glanced at Charlie and amended my word—"this over to Sheriff Clump."

"I get it," Sofi said, softly, glancing at her own daughter. "They weren't ready to let go."

I nodded agreement. "On top of that, there's Pops's job. If Clump takes this case, it will put him in a great position to maneuver a contract to police Red Jacket."

"Pops wouldn't want you to put yourself in danger, Hatti."

"I'm not in danger." I was shocked at the thought. "Not at all."

"You will be if you can identify a murderer."

The prospect should have shocked me, but since I couldn't put a face to the murderer it didn't really frighten me.

"I'll be careful."

Sofi's blue eyes, so much like my own, held my gaze for a minute. She'd always been a great older sister, mainly because she knew when to back off.

"What do you know so far?"

I told them. "The weirdest thing is what she was wearing. I can't come up with a single, logical reason for her to have put that costume back on."

"Maybe she was role-playing," Sofi said.

"Role-playing?"

She meant sexual role-playing. I was silent, wondering how to discuss this possibility in front of a fifteen-year-old.

"She had a sore throat," I pointed out, well aware that teenage hormones could always trump a trifling illness. Sofi, whose shotgun wedding had occurred during her last year of high school, knew it, too.

"Matti Murso is in love with her," Charlie offered, obviously comprehending at least some of our exchange. "Was in love, I should say."

"Diane Hakala told me yesterday that Liisa had only gone out with him once."

Charlie nodded. "The homecoming dance. He kept hoping, though. He walked her home a lot and stuff."

"That sounds pretty not serious," I said. They both nodded. "Who were Liisa's friends? At school, I mean."

"She didn't have any friends," Charlie said, with the cruel honesty of youth.

"That's sad."

Charlie shrugged. "I don't think she cared about that. I'm not even sure she cared about what she did to the guys."

"What do you mean?"

"When she walked down the hallway at school, guys stopped to stare at her. Not just classmates. Even Mr. Jokinen, the principal, and Mr. Evers, the music teacher."

"She was beautiful," Sofi admitted. "Maybe too beautiful. Looks like that can be dangerous. Look at Elizabeth Taylor."

"What happened to her?" Charlie asked.

I bypassed the issues Sofi had meant, including the multiple marriages, and responded literally.

"She died."

Charlie nodded. "Just like Liisa."

CHAPTER SIX

Sofi and her daughter went back to work, and I searched for a quiet corner at the festival so I could call Arvo, but there was no quiet corner. The place was teeming with visitors, which meant that *Pikkujoulu* was a success. I zipped up my parka and slipped out a side entrance. The cold, fresh air felt good on my face and soothed the jitters caused by multiple cups of coffee. I could get something to eat at home and let Larry out at the same time.

I dialed Arvo's cell and heard men talking and laughing in the background.

"Where are you?"

"The Nugget." It was the casino out on the Copper Eagle Reservation. "The guys from Lansing had enough crafts and pasties."

I guessed that made sense.

"Where do we stand on the Snow Train?"

"No problem. It's in the bag."

It was exactly what I'd have expected him to say, but his words lacked the shimmering good humor that usually surrounded Arvo's words. Liisa's death had knocked the stuffing out of him.

"Have you spoken with Jalmer Pelonen?"

A burst of laughter filled the receiver, then it faded.

"No. He doesn't answer his phone. He must be out on the lake. He goes every year at this time. Like clockwork."

I shivered, thinking of the loner who was undoubtedly happy as a clam in his snug little fishing hut on frozen Lake Gogebic and about the terrible news that awaited him.

"Somebody should go down there and find him."

Arvo heaved a heartfelt sigh. "I will do it tomorrow, Hatti-girl," he said, quietly. The voices in the background faded further, as if he were cupping his hand around the phone. "You should see her, Hatti. I covered the gash with her hair. She looks so beautiful. Like a saint. Like she could sit up and open those beautiful eyes and start singing."

My heart ached for him even as I sincerely hoped she wouldn't sit up and sing, and I knew he shouldn't have disturbed the body. I bit back the chastisement that sprang to my lips. I had known all along that Arvo wouldn't be able to leave his beloved Liisa sprawled on the sauna floor.

"Sonya is coming over to take a look at her."

He didn't seem to hear me. "I wanted to put her in the white Excelsior. It has little rosebuds carved into the sides, but I have waited. She's still in the embalming room."

"Embalming room?" I felt a surge of panic. When and if this case was handed over to the authorities, they would not be amused to find the body already embalmed.

"Just resting there. Just waiting. I haven't done anything but take off the candles and fix her hair. Not even changed her clothes. My beautiful *tytto.*"

"Thank you." I didn't know why I was thanking him except I knew it had taken a superhuman effort not to fix her up yet. I resisted the urge to remind him that Liisa Pelonen had not been his daughter, his *tytto.* "Will you be at the church for the pageant?"

"*Joo.* Of course."

"Is Pauline with you? I need to speak with her."

"She went to Elli's, then to *Pikkujoulu.*"

So I'd missed her. Well, there was nothing surprising about that. It occurred to me that the festival was really getting in the way of this investigation. Had that been part of the calculations? Had the murderer, hoping to escape detection by obscuring the facts, planned to kill the girl during the festival? If there was a murder. I fantasized for a few seconds about discovering this really was just an accident, but I couldn't believe it. No Finnish girl would faint in a sauna. Besides, she hadn't gone there to bathe. She'd been fully clothed in the St. Lucy costume.

What I'd give for a little Sherlockian insight, I thought, as I lifted my face to a fresh snowfall, or a few of Poirot's little gray cells. I had no idea of how to proceed.

I breathed deeply and slowly as I turned onto Third, then again onto Calumet Street. It wasn't until I was in front of the Makis' that I got a flash of inspiration. Where better to start than the scene of the crime?

The milk chute had been painted to match the rest of the funeral home, so it was practically invisible against the darkened brick, but I located it near the kitchen and chuckled when I found the key inside. I felt a mixture of excitement and trepidation as I let myself in. The foyer was dark and daunting, and I was uncomfortably aware that while I was not the only one in the house, I was the only one still breathing. I found myself holding that breath as I moved past Arvo's office and the embalming room and down the shadowed hall. The Makis lived upstairs, and I knew Pauline had recently updated that kitchen. The first-floor kitchen, though, still had the old linoleum floor, Formica countertops and even an ancient Norge. There were four doors in one corner of the room, one of which led to the backstairs, another to the basement, a third to the back porch and the fourth one to the greenhouse.

I felt the same sense of relief that I had the previous night when I stepped into the glass enclosed structure. It wasn't just the earthy, living scents that cheered me up. It was the light from the panels that covered the roof and sides. I glanced up at the falling flakes, and, for a minute, I felt like I'd stumbled into a snow globe. It wasn't an unpleasant sensation.

In that moment, I understood why Pauline had been so anxious to build the greenhouse in the space between the house and the sauna. A greenhouse was full of life and color, the perfect antidote to the dreariness of a funeral home. I'd intended to pass through to the sauna but found myself leaving the main aisle and detouring down the side paths, admiring the ferns and plants, the flowers and bonsai trees. There was a workstation in the back, complete with a laptop, a pegboard full of gardening tools, rakes, clippers, trowels, twine, a box of rubber hospital gloves, stacks of clay pots and a plastic organizer with rows of labeled bottles. I peered at the names: Liquid seaweed, Thrive Alive, Nitrogen, Phosphorous, Potassium, Sulfur, Advil. *Advil?* I picked up a jar of salve and almost dropped it when I heard the creak of the opening door.

"Hatti?" Pauline's voice sounded almost accusing, and I was embarrassed and ashamed for invading her privacy.

"Arvo said you were at the festival," I said, realizing I should have apologized. "I wanted to take another look at the crime scene."

She nodded, as if she understood. "But why are you in my greenhouse?"

I shrugged. "I've never been here before. It's lovely."

Her stern expression softened. "Would you like a tour?"

I set the Vicks on the countertop. I knew I should be pressing ahead with the investigation, but I really was curious about this place, Pauline's secret world. Not that it was really a secret. Everyone knew about it, and, in fact, she often provided flowers for Sofi's arrangements.

"I'd love one."

She pointed out the section where she started seedlings and the tables of plants that had reached maturity. She showed me succulents and the section of yellow roses, daisies and lilies. "My funeral flowers," she said. I nodded. Finns prefer yellow and white flowers for funerals. I wandered toward another table. "What's this?"

"Blue mystique orchid. It's a hybrid."

I lifted my brows. "Did you create it?"

Her smile was self-deprecating. "With the help of some special technology. Arvo calls it my 'robot orchid.' "

I laughed. "And this violet-blue flower?"

"An iris hybrid. I did that one the old fashioned way—with grafting. You can't graft just anything. There are compatibility markers."

"Next thing we know there will be plant marriage counselors."

"That's not as far out as it seems. There are some botanists who believe plants have emotions and even memories. Take nightshade," she said, pointing to a row of velvety midnight purplish blossoms with tiny berries. "A hundred years ago a scholar hypothesized that nightshade is so deadly because it harbors a lot of anger."

I felt a shiver work its way down my spine, but I chuckled.

"That's a little alarming, given the carnivorous plants, like Venus flytrap."

Pauline nodded. "Plants, like every other species, need a way to protect themselves. Some are carnivores, many are poisonous. Nightshade is also called *Atropa bella donna,* because centuries ago Italian women squeezed the juice out of the roots and used it to dilate their eyes, a mark of beauty."

I shivered. "Beautiful women and a deadly poison all in the same flower."

"A lot of people would say the two are not incompatible."

She pointed to a cluster of flowers. "Those are blue moon phlox."

"You seem to favor blue flowers."

"They're Arvo's favorites," she said, simply. "Blue for Finland."

Arvo might have brought an outsider to the Keweenaw, but he'd have been hard-pressed to find anyone who was more devoted than Pauline.

"Your plants all look so healthy," I said, "and I couldn't help noticing the pharmacy." I pointed to the collection of bottles and tubes.

"Most of those are supplements designed to enrich the soil, and there are a few concoctions intended to nurture sick plants."

"What about the drugstore stuff? Do plants get headaches?"

Pauline smiled serenely. "Some of those remedies are for me, but plants definitely suffer from too much stress. I try to keep anger and anxiety out of here."

"I can tell. It feels like a sanctuary."

"Yes. That's exactly what it is."

I thought suddenly of a W. H. Auden poem I'd studied in English Lit. It was titled, "As I Walked out One Morning," and it used the image of "a crack in the teacup" as a metaphor for the sanctuary we all need, a defense against the frightening abyss. I felt I understood her better than I had before.

"It can't have been easy to come up here to live," I said. She made no comment at the apparent non-sequitur.

"It's not so bad. Luckily, I don't mind snow."

"I don't mean that. We have such a closed community. I wasn't aware of it until I came home from D.C. last year. Have you been made to feel like an outsider?"

She shook her head. "No. Not really. But then, I married Red Jacket's favorite son."

There was a false note in her words, and I felt ashamed for

my community. Pauline had been accepted as Arvo's wife, but she had not been embraced for herself. I wondered absently if things would have been different if she and Arvo had had children. Not that it mattered now.

She peered at me, and I got the impression she read my thoughts.

"I chose my life here, Hatti. I've been happy with it."

A remarkable woman, Pauline Maki. I had a whole new appreciation for her.

I realized I'd gotten pretty far afield.

"Could I take a few more minutes of your time? I'd like to compile a kind of timeline of yesterday."

The calm and contentment of the past few minutes seemed to evaporate, leaving a weary middle-aged woman with a long, drawn face, deep circles under her eyes and a set of grim lines bracketing her lips.

"Of course. Let's sit down." We sat on one of the long benches, and I dug into my purse for a notebook and pencil.

"Could you start with the morning? What time did Liisa get up?"

"She got up at six."

I blinked. "Six? On a day when there was no school?"

"We always get up at six. It's part of our routine."

I wrote down "got up at six." "Then what?"

"Let's see. I made her breakfast: scrambled eggs, fresh orange juice and bacon. Oh, and *korvapuustit*," she added, referring to the cinnamon rusks that are commonly dunked in coffee.

"Do you always cook like that in the morning?"

"Sometimes we just have cereal. Yesterday was special." Pauline's voice quavered.

"Because it was St. Lucy Day?"

"And her birthday. Liisa turned eighteen."

I sucked in my breath. Liisa Pelonen had died on her

birthday. Somehow, that made it so much worse.

"After breakfast," Pauline continued, without prompting, "Liisa and Arvo left to string more lights downtown. She was supposed to go from there to pageant rehearsal at one."

"What happened?" I asked, although I'd already heard this story.

"She didn't get there. Not until just before the parade."

That was nearly two hours unaccounted for. Maybe more. I'd have to find out when she'd left Arvo.

"Where was she?" I sensed this was a critical piece of information and held my breath even though I knew Pauline wouldn't have the answer.

"She'd gone down to the Frostbite Mall in Houghton," Pauline said easily. "She was looking for something to wear to the Snowflake Dance last night." She shook her head sadly. "She could have saved the trip."

"Did she go alone?"

"She had no transportation. She must have gone with a friend."

A friend? According to Charlie, Liisa had no friends.

"Do you know who?"

Pauline shook her head. "All I know is that she asked Arvo if she could leave around eleven A.M., and she promised to be back for the pageant rehearsal." She sighed. "You know girls once they start shopping."

I certainly knew that girls liked to shop. I liked to shop.

"So what did she get?"

"Pardon?"

"At the mall. What did she get to wear to the dance?"

The somber look in Pauline's hazel eyes turned bleak.

"I don't know. I never thought to ask. First, I was angry that she'd missed the rehearsal, and then she was sick, and then, and then . . ." Her voice trailed off, and I decided to take pity on her.

"Of course."

"After the parade," Pauline soldiered on, "we came home, and she complained of a sore throat. She had a fever, too. I offered to stay home from the smorgasbord, but she said she wouldn't need me. She was just going to go to sleep. I tucked her in, and that's where she was when I came back for the jam." She shook her head. "But, somehow, between six-thirty and nine o'clock, she got into that infernal costume and got herself killed." Pauline's hands came up to cover her face. "I should have stayed home with her. May God forgive me. I don't think I will ever be able to forgive myself."

"Oh, Pauline." I wanted to gather her into my arms, but I knew she wouldn't welcome the gesture. In her own way, Pauline was as self-contained as Liisa's real father, the hermit. "How did you know where to look for her?"

She lifted her head. "Arvo panicked when she wasn't in her room. We searched the upstairs and downstairs. We came in here, and finally, because there was no place else to look, we went into the sauna."

"And you have no idea why she was wearing the costume."

"None."

"Did Liisa have any enemies? Anyone who would wish her harm?"

"No. None." She paused. "Ronja Laplander wasn't really her biggest fan."

An understatement. But I still thought the idea of stolid, earthbound, mother-of-five Ronja as murderer was improbable.

"I know Ronja wasn't really mad at the child," Pauline said. "It was just that Liisa's extraordinary beauty put people's backs up, made them jealous."

The hair on the back of my neck tingled. Jealousy was at the root of this, I was sure of it. Well, pretty sure.

"Behind that perfect face was a kind and loving girl," Pauline went on. "No one could have hated her enough to kill her."

Except that someone had.

CHAPTER SEVEN

I asked for permission to search Liisa's room and Pauline hesitated. I got the feeling she didn't want anyone rifling through Liisa's belongings, invading her space. But, as always with Pauline, common sense took over. I was, after all, supposed to be investigating Liisa's suspicious death.

She led me out of the greenhouse, into the kitchen and up the backstairs that had been built for servants back in the day. Our house had a similar setup.

I had never been on the Makis' second floor, and I was somehow shocked at the cool beauty of the spacious living room with its pristine white walls, polished walnut floor, rattan furniture upholstered in a bright green, leafy pattern and sophisticated indirect lighting. A Marimekko abstract of emerald green leaves and bright red poppies dominated one wall. The room belonged in an upscale beach house, not in a U.P. funeral home.

"I call it my Florida room," Pauline explained, noting my astonishment. "Isn't that silly way up here in the north? I find the colors soothing somehow."

"It's beautiful, Pauline," I said truthfully. Reminiscent of the greenhouse.

She nodded to acknowledge the compliment and indicated a closed door.

"That's Liisa's room, but if you're looking for clues, you won't find much. I certainly didn't find anything when I cleaned it this morning."

I sighed, inwardly. I should have asked Pauline and Arvo not to touch anything. Already the body had been moved and interfered with, and the murder site and the girl's room had been cleaned. If I'd been a real detective, I'd have warned them against that.

Concern about my investigative shortcomings flew out of my head the minute I entered the bedroom. Just for an instant, I felt as if I'd stepped into someone's mouth. At first I thought everything was pink—Pepto Bismol pink—but as I looked around I realized the furniture, including the four-poster-canopied bed, was white. Everything else, though, from the canopy to the chenille bedspread to the thick carpet on the floor looked as if it had come out of a Double Bubble wrapper. Even the brand-new jewelry box on the dressing table and the little dancer inside.

I felt like I was inside a four-year-old's birthday cake.

What had happened to Pauline's vaunted judgment? What had happened to the excellent taste that had created the Florida room? I soon found out.

"I felt so fortunate when I found out Liisa was coming to live here," Pauline said, a quaver in her voice. "After all these years I was getting a chance to create a fantasy room for a child."

A color-blind child, I thought, or, for that child's surrogate mother.

"It's very feminine," I said, diplomatically, "and I'm sure she loved it."

Pauline nodded and sniffed. "I'll leave you to it."

As soon as the door closed behind her, I crossed the room to the jewelry box. I wound the key and watched the ballerina pirouette to a tinny version of "Somewhere, Over the Rainbow." There was a set of pink pearls inside: necklace, earrings and bracelet arranged on the pink velvet lining. I suspected Pauline had given them to Liisa for the Homecoming Dance. I removed the top tray, but found nothing at all in the lower part of the box. Next, I opened the dresser drawers. Fresh, new-looking underwear, nightgowns and sweaters were carefully folded. I crossed to the closet, where I found blouses buttoned on the hangers, neatly pressed slacks, several jackets and a pale pink floor-length dress with a ruffled neckline that even Charlie, who was not at all interested in dances or in fashion, would have judged to be too young. There were dozens of boxes of shoes and a neat line of purses along the shelf.

My first reaction was disappointment. Nothing in the room gave a clue about the dead girl. There were no photos, no posters, no pom-poms or magazines or even books to reveal her personality. A moment later I realized I was wrong. True, she hadn't left a footprint of herself, but the room revealed something about her surrogate parents. They had wanted a child, and they had welcomed Liisa Pelonen as if she represented the Second Coming. They'd loved her. I felt a jolt of compassion that nearly knocked me over.

A distant clock chimed, and I realized it was getting late. I found Pauline seated on the neatly made bed in her own room. She was staring at a picture. Liisa was smiling, looking into the warmth of Arvo Maki's blue eyes. They looked like father and daughter. Had Pauline Maki, with her plain brown hair and eyes, felt like an outsider? I thought not. I hoped not. There was anguish on her long face.

"You've got to be exhausted," I said. "Why don't you stay here and rest?"

She shook her head. "Arvo will be expecting me."

St. Heikki's Finnish Lutheran was the more elaborate of Red Jacket's two Gothic cathedrals. In addition to its flying buttresses, it had a soaring spire and leaded glass windows and gargoyles under the eaves. Sofi, with her penchant for *le mot juste,* called it the perfect summer house for the Hunchback of Notre Dame. I sat next to Arvo and Pauline in the narthex while a dozen girls ranging from kindergarten to twelfth grade and dressed in white robes and red sashes processed up the aisle to the dais in the chancel to join the substitute St. Lucy.

In contrast to Liisa Pelonen's ethereal beauty, Astrid Laplander, with her square face, cube-shaped body and short, dark hair, was distinctly earthbound. Even the lighted crown of candles failed to draw any luminescence from her heavy features, but, as I glanced at the glow on Ronja's face, I knew that, for at least one Red Jacket family, a perceived wrong had been righted by last night's shocking event. And it wasn't just a perceived wrong. Tradition was the backbone of our town, and Arvo never should have bypassed it.

The organ swelled with the familiar melody, and the girls began to sing the traditional, haunting words.

> *The evening is beautiful,*
> *little breeze blows fresh and light.*
> *Or to be late? The evening is beautiful.*
> *Come quickly my boat,*
> *Saint Lucy! Saint Lucy!*

I glanced at the couple next to me and was startled to see that Arvo's arm was around his wife and her head was on his shoulder. Like most of us on the Keweenaw, they did not often indulge in public displays of affection. Today, they were clearly drawing comfort from one another, and I felt tears prick the backs of my eyes. And then Arvo glanced at me, and I mouthed a message: *I need to talk to you.* He nodded.

After the pageant, the Makis and I made our way down the

stone steps to the basement, where Pauline joined the women of the Martha Circle, who were setting up punch, coffee and plates of pastries including *joulutorttu*. Arvo and I continued down a narrow corridor to the church parlor, in use today as a green room. Coats, jackets, boots and mittens littered the shabby furniture, and there were empty juice cartons and food wrappers everywhere. I figured it would take the parents about ten minutes to greet each other, to accept congratulations on behalf of the young performers and to consume the refreshments before they interrupted us. Arvo didn't wait for me to speak.

"Any progress?"

I shook my head. "I took a look at Liisa's room. There was no help there. In fact," I added, eyeing him curiously, "there was nothing personal there at all."

A look of surprise flashed across his face. "I never noticed, eh? When I was in her room I wasn't aware of anything but her."

The words frustrated me. I couldn't seem to get a handle on the girl whose death I was supposed to investigate.

"I'd like to understand her better," I said.

"There was no great mystery, Hatti. She was just a girl. A beautiful angel of a girl, eh? It is so hard for me to believe she is gone."

I tried another tack.

"How often did she use the sauna?"

"Not so much. She said she had never liked it much. In that way, she and Pauly were alike."

"Were they alike in other ways? Did Liisa like to hang out with Pauline in the greenhouse?"

"She didn't like the smells," he said. "She preferred to spend her evenings in the office."

"Your office?" I could hardly believe that a girl who hadn't

73

liked the scents in a greenhouse would be comfortable with those associated with embalming.

"She liked to type things for me and to file. And we talked."

Finally I was getting somewhere. "Talked about what?"

"Her dreams. She wanted to become a famous singer."

"Did she talk to you about her friends?"

"Her friends?"

"Other kids from school. Boys."

"Of course."

"Can you remember any of their names?"

He frowned in an effort at memory. "Matti. Barb Hakala, I think. The usual kids at school."

"Was she dating Matti?"

"Oh, no. Just for the homecoming dance."

"Was she dating anyone else?"

"*Ei*. I don't think so."

Once again the essence of Liisa Pelonen eluded me.

"It must be an accident," Arvo said, finally. "No one could want to kill her. I will call Sheriff Clump."

He was letting me off the hook. I should have been thrilled or, at least, relieved, but I wasn't. I might be frustrated, but I wasn't defeated. Cripes, I hadn't even heard from Sonya yet.

"Let me have until tomorrow evening," I said, holding up my hands when it was clear he intended to argue with me. "I'll admit it might turn out to be an accident, but let me ask a few more questions. Remember, Clump wants to take over our town, and he'll use this incident to do it. Let me save Pops's job."

He eyed me with some curiosity.

"I thought you were not qualified to investigate?"

"I'm not. But I'm interested now. I want to find out what really happened to Liisa, not just brush it under the rug."

It was an inspired argument, since Arvo knew as well as

anybody that Clump always took the easiest path.

Voices in the hall outside our door warned of the returning thespians, which worked to my advantage. There was no more time to argue.

"One more day," I murmured as the noises in the hallway erupted into the parlor.

His lips tipped into a half-smile. "You are stubborn—like your *isa.*"

My cell phone rang, and I slipped into the hallway to answer it.

"You'd better come over to the funeral home," Sonya said. "I've found something."

My stomach clenched, but with excitement, not panic. Finally, a clue. As I agreed, a hand on my shoulder sent shivers wiggling up my spine. I forced myself to look and let out a sigh of relief as I realized it was only Pauline.

"Can you give me a ride home?" she asked.

It occurred to me that she, too, would be interested to hear what Sonya had to say.

When we got to the side door, I realized it was snowing heavily now. Pauline, for the first time I could remember, looked frail.

"Let me get the Jeep. I'll bring it up to the door so you won't get wet," I said, then disappeared into the parking lot before she could argue.

I lowered my head against a fresh blast of snow and headed toward the Jeep parallel parked down by the firehouse. Just as I reached the door, I heard my name uttered in a deeply attractive masculine voice. My heart fluttered as I watched the masculine entity in a Dennis Weaver–type cowboy hat saunter in my direction.

"You look like an angel."

I'd have melted at that description if Arvo hadn't just used the same words to describe a dead girl.

"Like you just flew off the top of a Christmas tree."

He was eyeing me strangely, as if I had whipped cream on my face.

"Hatti? Anything wrong?"

And then I remembered what Sonya had said about Max Guthrie's background.

"As a matter of fact, there is. Not with me," I said, catching the quick flash of concern on his rugged features. "I'd like to talk to you about something though, when you have time."

"How 'bout tonight?"

"After the smorgasbord," I suggested. "At my house. Around nine?"

He nodded. "I'll bring the wine." He winked. "And doughnuts for breakfast."

His long lashes, so incongruous in the masculine face, dipped, an action that maximized the effect of his bedroom eyes. I felt a flutter of anticipation followed by a pang of guilt. This wasn't going to be an assignation. Was it?

Sonya greeted Pauline and me at the funeral home's front door. I was struck, as always, by the midwife's serene beauty. Her eyes appeared as dark as her hair until she stepped into the light and they were revealed as an inky blue. Her complexion was soft and creamy despite her thirty-five years, and her hair gleamed, straight and dark. There was a frown on the lovely face.

"I think we'll be more comfortable upstairs," Pauline said, leading us. "I'll make some tea."

Sonya's hesitation was instant and quickly overcome, but I knew she'd have preferred to speak with me privately. A few minutes later Pauline handed us each a hand-thrown pottery mug filled with fragrant chamomile tea. It occurred to me that if she had been Finnish, she'd have offered coffee. Suddenly, I couldn't wait another minute for information.

"Was it an accident?"

The midwife shook her head. "I don't think so."

I could feel Pauline's tension. Or maybe it was mine.

"I believe she was hit with the sauna rock, but the cut wasn't deep, and there was very little blood." She looked at me. "I think she was hit after she died."

That didn't seem to make sense.

"But then how did she die?"

Sonya shrugged. "I couldn't find anything. A coroner probably could. Remember, I have no access to a lab."

I bit my lip. The information was just confusing.

"Why would someone hit her after she was dead?"

Sonya shook her head, but her eyes were on Pauline, who had become very pale.

"Is that it? Is that all you found?"

Sonya hesitated, her eyes revealing concern. "Not all. I think you should brace yourself for a shock, Pauline. I did an internal exam. Her uterus was enlarged."

I stared at my friend. "What does that mean?"

Sonya glanced at me. "It means she was pregnant." She looked back at the older woman. "About six weeks."

Pauline's mug bounced on the floor, spilling tea everywhere. The mug itself didn't break. Sonya and I jumped out of our chairs and hurried to her side. I picked up one of her hands and found it ice cold.

"That's simply not possible. I mean, she couldn't have been pregnant. She never had anything to do with boys."

Except for the night she went to the homecoming dance with Barb Hakala's boyfriend. Six weeks earlier.

Pauline was breathing hard, and Sonya helped her to her feet.

"I'm going to put her into bed," Sonya said. "Bring her a glass of water, Hatti."

My first thought, as we tended to Pauline's immediate needs, was that I now had a viable prime suspect. But my second was more cautious. Six weeks was early to know about a pregnancy. It was possible that Liisa herself didn't know and likely that Matti was completely in the dark. If he didn't know about the baby, there was no motive for him to kill Sonya.

Pauline let Sonya lead her into the bedroom, but once there, she grabbed the midwife's sleeve.

"Please," she begged, "don't tell Arvo about this. It would break his heart."

"I won't," Sonya said, automatically honoring the request of a patient. I could make no such promise. The pregnancy might or might not be related to Liisa's death, but it was unquestionably a significant development.

Pauline refused to stay in bed, so we waited for her to wash her face and repair her makeup before we went down the street to the B&B. We turned Pauline over to her husband and reported to the kitchen, where Elli assigned me to serve ham and prunes, while Sonya got the *kulta salantti,* or golden salad composed of carrots, mandarin oranges, orange juice and honey. Sofi was there, too, scooping helpings of corn pudding and calico beans onto plates. Next to her, Charlie was in charge of the tender whitefish filets called *mojakka.*

The dining room was filled with lively chatter about the festival and the St. Lucy pageant. I heard several people asking Pauline whether Liisa was on the mend. She always replied in a vague manner but with polite friendliness. I glanced across the room at Diane Hakala, tonight accompanied by her husband and daughter, and wondered what Liisa's death and her pregnancy would mean to that family. The Laplanders were present to receive accolades on Astrid's performance. Ronja beamed with unaccustomed good humor.

Was I really considering these people I'd known all my life as serious murder suspects?

I tried to approach the problem from another angle. I'd been trying to find out about Liisa Pelonen and had, until now, come up empty. The pregnancy, however, cast a new light on her. She was not the docile girl who stayed home at night to help her surrogate father with his books. At least, she hadn't been on one night. It was something. It was time, I thought, to pay a little visit to Matti Murso.

After supper, Sonya found me in the kitchen with Sofi. We were drying the last few pieces of Elli's Christmas china.

I made sure all the knitters knew about the baby, but when I'd finished, Sonya continued to look grave.

"There's something else, Hatti. I didn't mention it before because, well, I just didn't. Liisa was wearing something around her neck."

I perked up at the thought of another clue.

"What? What was it?"

Sonya reached into the pocket of her jeans and pulled out a fine copper chain strung with an intricately made charm, which she dropped into my hand.

Sofi lifted it into the air to get a better look. "Pretty," she said. "So delicate. I've never seen anything like this before. What is it?"

"A dream catcher," I said, hoarsely.

"That's right," Sonya agreed. "The spider web in the middle of the hoop is intended to catch and hold bad dreams, and the feathers dangling on the bottom transport the good dreams back to the sleeping child. Once the sun rises, the bad dreams disappear."

"Hatti," Elli said, concern in her voice, "you look kinda funny. You've seen this pendant before, haven't you?"

"Last year. On my dresser in D.C. Jace gave it to me the day we were married. I left it behind."

"Bad associations," Sonya asked, sympathetically.

"It's a family heirloom. It belongs to the Night Winds."

Sofi and Elli exchanged a look, and my sister said, "In that case, what was it doing around the dead girl's neck?"

CHAPTER EIGHT

The wind had turned the falling snow into a riot of flying Frisbees, but I was barely aware of the attack as I made my way across the yard to the Queen Anne. All my senses were focused on the past, that pitiless Sunday when I'd left behind what I'd thought was my future.

As an attorney specializing in laws that applied to Native Americans, Jace spent a lot of time flying to reservations around the country. My status as a law school dropout qualified me to manage the office and his handful of volunteers. I was proud of the work he did and of my own contribution to it, and I didn't object to his frequent absences.

In the weeks before our first Christmas, he'd flown out to the Pine Ridge Reservation in South Dakota, home of the Oglala Sioux, to handle a case, and, unknown to me, he'd stopped off at the Copper Eagle to see his grandfather, Chief Joseph, and his younger, half-brother, Reid. During the year after our breakup, I wondered why he'd kept that trip a secret, but I'd never found out. I'd never even found out why he'd returned to D.C. and abruptly ended our marriage.

I'd decorated our apartment with a fresh pine tree and handmade ornaments from both of our cultures. I had *joulu-tortu*, the prune tarts served during the holidays, as well as the fry bread he remembered from his childhood, and I had turned our radio to a station playing a variety of Christmas music. When I heard his key in the lock, I'd just finished listening to

81

"Grandma Got Run Over by a Reindeer." In retrospect, it seemed apt, even though I'm not and never will be a grandmother.

I flew to the foyer and launched myself into his arms the way I always did when he'd been away overnight. He caught me in his arms as usual, but it felt different. I could hear both of our hearts thudding in our chests, but he hadn't buried his face in my long hair, and there was no intense kiss, no murmur of welcome. The tension that had turned his lean, muscular body into a tightwire was not, unfortunately, sexual in nature.

I stepped back and looked up into the gray eyes that could reveal intelligent comprehension, amusement, compassion and blazing heat. Today, though, they were as flat as the dark agates Elli and I sometimes collected on the shores of Lake Superior. His voice was flat, too.

"I'm sorry, Hatti."

He hadn't called me my actual name since the first week we'd met. I just looked at him, hoping my instincts were wrong.

They weren't.

"I'm sorry," he repeated. "It's over."

I felt like a fish caught in a frozen pond, a fly stuck in amber. I couldn't seem to move or think or speak. I was aware that he'd moved away from me, that he'd carried his canvas suitcase and the backpack that contained his computer into our bedroom. I was aware that he stayed in the bedroom unpacking and putting away his clothes. I was aware of another song on the radio: "All I Want for Christmas is My Two Front Teeth." Eventually, the shellshock wore off, and I confronted him, willing myself not to burst into tears or explode in anger.

"Jace. What are you talking about?"

I continued to ask for the next two days. Sometimes I screamed. Sometimes I cried. Sometimes I buried my head in a pillow for awhile, but when I emerged, I asked again for an explanation. I never got one. He listened to me. He didn't leave the room or turn his back, but he never fought back or argued. He never lost his temper at all, which was how I knew it really was over.

That Sunday I threw a few clothes and books into the back-seat of the Jeep and started the long, dismal December trip back to Michigan.

My mother, who had never approved of my precipitous marriage, wanted the explanation I didn't have. It was Pops, dear, understanding Pops, who protected me. He allowed me two months of wallowing, and then he handed over the keys to his bait shop, saying that he wanted to spend his time with my mother and as Red Jacket's part-time police chief. He set up a payment plan so that I'd be able to buy the shop if I decided I wanted it, and he supported my decision to add yarn and knitting supplies. My sister, cousin and new friend Sonya were my support system during that time and after, but I always felt it was Pops who'd saved my sanity.

A few weeks before his accident, he told me I'd received several letters from Jace's bank, all of them checks.

"I have them here, Hatti-girl," he'd said. "What do you want me to do with them, eh?"

"Tear them up."

He chuckled. "Consider it done."

I knew that eventually I'd have to file for divorce—or he would—but I wasn't in a hurry. It wasn't like I would marry again. I was happy at home, happy not hearing from Jace. I was just plain happy. Until Sonya Stillwater placed the dream catcher in my palm.

I was too busy struggling with my feelings at first, but by the time I'd waded through the knee-high snow, I'd begun to realize what was going on. The pendant connected the murder to my husband.

The heavy, wet snow had turned my hair to seaweed. My sodden parka seemed to weigh a ton, and I shivered as I slogged up the steps of the front porch. I'd failed to leave a light on, but as I hadn't bothered to lock the door, it wasn't a problem. I wrenched off my mittens and reached for the big, brass knob, when I felt a sudden, creepy awareness that I was not alone. My instinct was to race into the house, slam the door behind me and lock it. I forced myself instead (partly because my fingers were too cold to turn the knob) to look over my shoulder at the darkest corner of the porch. Something large, masculine and intimidating materialized from the shadows. The hairs stood up on the back of my neck, and my heart ping-ponged in my chest, until I remembered my appointment with Max. I was a little sorry now. A trained cop would quickly make the connection between the dream catcher and the rez, and I really, really, really didn't want to go down that path. I managed what would have been a poor excuse for a smile if there'd been any light.

"You should have gone inside," I said, trying to remember that I'd invited him here and that he was a friend.

"You left the door unlocked? Are you insane?"

The growled response was distinctly unfriendly, but friendship had never played a part in my relationship with Jace Night Wind.

I held very still as a coldness that had nothing to do with the December night seemed to fill the cavity behind my nose. I fought the rising panic as I felt his body—lean, powerful and familiar—against my own back. He reached around me to open the door, then nudged me to the side so he could enter first.

I was grateful for the resentment that flared inside me. So much better than panic.

"Hold on," I said, as he strode through the door. "You can't come in. I'm expecting company." He ignored that and flipped on the foyer light, enabling me to see that the fingers of his left hand were curled around a bottle. "That's his wine, isn't it? Where's Max? What did you do to him?"

I found myself staring at the black leather jacket, suitable for autumn weekends in Virginia but as out of place on the Keweenaw as a yachting windbreaker. It emphasized his wide shoulders just as the worn jeans hugged his lean hips and long legs. The soft light turned the snow in his hair to glitter and emphasized the harsh lines of his uncompromising features. I felt a surge of the old magic, but now I resented it.

"He left," Jace said. His gray eyes were unrevealing. "After I told him you were married. Apparently, that was news."

"I have more news for you," I said, through gritted teeth. "I've filled out divorce papers. As long as you're here, I'd like you to sign them." Part of that had the merit of being true. I definitely wanted him to sign them.

The steady gaze didn't falter, but I sensed a new tension and knew exactly what it was. He'd come for closure. He'd probably brought his own papers. When he spoke he surprised me again.

"Got anything to eat?"

I wanted to say there was no food in the house or in Red Jacket, that he wasn't welcome here, that he should turn around and snowshoe back to D.C. Unfortunately, I knew how long it took to get here (at least three connecting flights or twenty hours on the road), and I could see the fatigue in the lines scoring his cheeks and the shadows under his eyes. He undoubtedly was hungry as well as exhausted, and we on the Keweenaw are nothing if not hospitable.

I glared at him but started down the hallway toward the kitchen. An instant later I felt a hand burning my shoulder.

"Take off your jacket and boots first," he said, "and for God's sake, Hatti, dry your hair. You look like a drowned rat."

Which was, when I thought about it, exactly how I felt, too.

A few minutes later we were in the kitchen, Jace sprawled on one of my mom's kitchen chairs. I plunked a mug of fresh coffee on the wicker table in front of him, then extracted a plate of tarts from the big tin breadbox on the counter. Jace popped an entire tart in his mouth with one hand. He used his other hand to offer a tart to Larry.

I glared at the basset hound, who remained at his feet as Jace scratched the soft places behind his long ears, but I knew I had to drop the hostility. The sooner we got our business finished, the sooner Jace would be gone again. I plopped down into another of the chairs.

"*Joulutorttu.* Did you make them?"

His gray eyes were so familiar, as was his gravelly voice and the scent of his soap. Something moved under my heart, and it took all my wherewithal to clamp down on it. I couldn't remember whether I'd made the tarts or not.

The dark eyebrows rose in a question I didn't seem to be able to answer. H-E-double hockey sticks. I'd figured I'd see him again someday, but not until I made the *New York Times* bestselling author list, was CEO of Google and married to Brad Pitt. I wasn't ready for this.

"You cut your hair."

I could feel the blood rush into my cheeks and knew there was no way he could miss it. I knew he'd know that I'd cut my waist-length hair out of grief.

"It's easier to take care of," I said, ungraciously, "and Max likes it." I had no idea whether Max liked it, but I hoped the mention of the other man might keep Jace from noticing and understanding my blush. It did. His eyes narrowed briefly, which gave me enough time to observe something.

"You cut your hair, too."

I'd loved the long, black silk of his unbound hair but had to admit that the neat, razored Don-Draper look emphasized his mile-high cheekbones and long dark lashes.

"It's more professional."

Therein, I thought, lay one difference between us. He was a young man on the move in the nation's capital, and I was stuck in my hometown in what wasn't even a fly-over state. No wonder the marriage hadn't survived.

"Speaking of professions, I hear you've got a new career."

I thought about trying to tell him about ordering boxes of fish hooks and sorting the brilliant jewel-toned skeins of yarn. He wouldn't be interested, and, sad to say, his lack of interest would diminish my own pride in my new life. I gave him the briefest possible answer.

"I've got a shop."

"I meant your job as top cop."

"Temporary top cop," I corrected him, automatically. "It's just till my dad returns from the Mayo."

And then he corrected me. "Your stepdad." I frowned, but he gave me no time to speak. "What happened to him?"

"Hit-and-run snowmobile accident. Lots of broken bones." I could see he was working on the last tart, so I stood. "I'll get the divorce papers, and you can be on your way."

His hand shot out so fast I had no time to react. His fingers closed around mine.

"Hang on, Umlaut." I had to hang on. I felt as if I'd stuck my finger in an electrical socket. It didn't help that he'd called me by the pet name. "I want to talk to you about the murder."

Geez Louise. He wasn't here to initiate the divorce; that was just a lucky byproduct. He was here because the dream-catcher pendant hadn't lied. There was a connection between Liisa Pelonen's murder and the rez. I couldn't help it. I laughed.

"What in the hell's funny about a murder?"

"Nothing. Nothing. So. You're here about the murder. How did you hear about it?"

"My grandfather called me. What do you know so far?"

I shook my head, slightly. I might be the world's biggest moron where my marriage was concerned, but I wasn't a complete fool. I knew it had taken him at least fifteen or sixteen hours to get here from D.C. The murder had been discovered only twenty-four hours ago. That meant that Chief Joseph had to have been one of the first to know about it, and I wanted to know why.

"Let's start," I drawled, "with what you know and how you learned it."

I thought I detected a flicker of respect in the gray eyes. I thought he might try to finesse more information out of me, but I shortchanged him. He was direct and honest.

"The girl was a friend of my brother's. Reid found her last night, and he told my grandfather."

The explanation made sense, but I felt a sudden weight on my chest. Did that mean that Reid Night Wind was the murderer?

"No," Jace said, reading my thoughts. "Reid was supposed to meet her at the Makis' sauna. They had a scheduled rendezvous. When he got there, around seven P.M., she was dead."

It was a hugely important piece of information, as it explained why Liisa had gotten out of bed to go to the sauna. I knew Jace's half brother was about twenty-one. If he'd inherited the same devastatingly attractive genes, I figured I had the answer to another of the investigation's troubling questions: who had fathered Liisa's baby?

"Why didn't he call the sheriff?"

The gray eyes registered disappointment with me.

"An Ojibwe kid who's already got a rap sheet? Clump would have had him locked up with no bail before I could have gotten out of D.C."

I hadn't known about Reid's priors, but I wasn't surprised. Their mother, Miriam Night Wind, had gotten pregnant at fifteen. She'd run away from the Copper Eagle and wound up raising Jace and, later, Reid on a Canadian rez, where she'd wound up as a drunken prostitute. The family had been tolerated but not accepted, and Jace had sometimes had to steal money for food. Later on, after their mother died, Jace had felt guilt over leaving Reid with Chief Joseph while he'd joined the Army and gotten an education. I'd known all this but had never considered how much damage had been done by the circumstances of those early years. No wonder he hadn't been able to sustain the intimacy of a marriage. No wonder he hadn't wanted to. I dragged my mind back to the issue at hand.

"Your brother's been in trouble before?"

"He got busted five years ago for running a cat lab up in the Porkies."

Methcathinone, or "cat," was the poor man's methamphetamine, and cat labs had proliferated in the U.P. during the past twenty years, partly because of the remote location and partly because the substance could be made using household items including lithium batteries, aquarium tubing, starter fluid, acetone and Gatorade bottles.

"He was cleared of that charge. He was also cleared in the other complaint," he added, with a slight grimace.

"The other charge?"

He didn't want to tell me. I waited, and he finally spoke.

"Paternity suit."

Hell's bells! Jace was right about one thing. Any real cop would have Reid Night Wind behind bars before the next snowfall. Without some kind of help, some mitigating circumstances, the discovery of someone else as murderer, Reid Night Wind was toast.

"He didn't kill her, Hatti."

"How do you know?"

"Grandfather believes him. Nobody ever puts anything over

on that old man. He's a shaman."

I hadn't known that. Information about Jace's family had filtered to me on a strictly, need-to-not-tell-me basis.

"You said Reid and Liisa were friends," I said, sticking to the point in what I thought was an admirable fashion. "Why were they planning to meet clandestinely?"

Jace ran his long, lean fingers through his hair. "The whole relationship was clandestine, apparently. He was helping her run away from Red Jacket. He'd found a place in Marquette."

"Liisa was running away?" For some reason, that possibility had never occurred to me. "Do you know why?"

"Probably the usual reasons."

"It couldn't have been because she didn't get enough attention. The Makis loved her as if she were their own daughter."

"Love isn't always enough."

My face stung as if I'd been slapped. In four words he'd summed up the problem with our marriage.

He tossed me another scrap of information as if to make up for hurting me.

"Reid said she was afraid of something or someone."

I didn't understand. "If she was afraid, why didn't she go to Arvo?"

"I don't know, Hatti. Maybe she was afraid of him."

Impossible. I kept the word to myself. It was impossible for me to believe anyone, much less Liisa Pelonen, could be afraid of bombastic, big-hearted Arvo Maki.

"I need to speak to Reid. Where is he now?"

"Up in the Porcupine Mountains. He went to stay in the cabin we built up there when we first came to the Copper Eagle."

I groaned, inwardly. It was a challenge for a non-woodswoman like me to hike up the forested Porkies in the summer. In the winter, with feet of snow covering everything and making footing unstable, it'd be all but impossible. But I'd have to try. Reid

Night Wind was rapidly emerging as my prime suspect.

"Tell me how to get there."

"Hold on," he said, again. "It's your turn to talk to me."

I opened my mouth but shut it again, quickly, as it became blindingly apparent that our interests, Jace's and mine, were likely to diverge. How much information did I want to share with him?

"Fair's fair, Umlaut," he said. "I've given you a lot. And, if it's any consolation, I don't think we'll wind up on opposite sides in this dogfight. Reid didn't kill her. You have my word on it."

His word, for once, wasn't enough, and we both knew it. Still, there seemed little point in withholding information, and I knew Jace wouldn't leave the Keweenaw until he'd established his brother's innocence. And then I knew, from all the court cases he'd handled, that he was a natural investigator, and I could use his help. The bits and pieces just didn't seem to add up.

I told him about Liisa's background, her childhood with the reclusive Jalmer, her goal of becoming a singer, the invitation from Arvo to live at the funeral home while she finished high school, and the affection that had grown between herself and her surrogate parents. I told him about the St. Lucy controversy, too, and about Matti Murso, the homecoming dance and Barb Hakala's disappointment.

"Whoever she was afraid of," I told him, "it couldn't have been Arvo or Pauline. I saw them the night they found her body. Both of them were devastated."

I paused, trying to decide whether to share the news about Sonya's autopsy. The gray eyes lidded.

"There's something else, isn't there? Something important?"

I wasn't surprised. He'd always been able to read me. Not that he'd had to employ the skill very often. In direct contrast to him, I'd pretty much told him everything that was on my mind. I held his gaze.

"Liisa was pregnant. Six weeks."

The short, harsh syllable that escaped him carried enough intensity to make Larry look up at him. I knew I'd surprised and distressed him, and I probably should have taken some pleasure in that. I didn't.

"There's been no official autopsy, of course, but Sonya Still-water is our local midwife and my friend. She looked over the body this afternoon."

He cursed again, but this time it was softer. Then he sprawled back in his chair in a deliberately casual position, but I wasn't fooled. The gray eyes flashed with intensity.

"Who?"

I shrugged. "As far as I know her only date was the Home-coming Dance on Halloween. Matti Murso had a big time crush on her, but she wasn't really interested."

"Halloween was six weeks ago," he said, unnecessarily.

"Believe it or not, I was able to figure that out for myself. I'll talk to him tomorrow right after I get back from the Porkies." And the conversation with my number one suspect.

"Does anyone know she was seeing my brother?"

My heart twisted. Surely he wasn't thinking about covering it up.

"I'm not that big a fool," he said, wearily, reading my mind again. "I just want to know how much time I have before all hell breaks loose."

I nodded. It was a reasonable question. I got up and padded into the foyer, retrieved the pendant and brought it back to the kitchen. I let the fine chain slide through my fingers like liquid copper. It coiled into a little mound on the oilcloth surface.

Jace's eyes were on the necklace. I could tell the precise moment he recognized it. Another coarse word exploded from his mouth.

"Sonya found this when she examined the body. I don't think the Makis knew she had it. I don't know about anybody else."

The gray eyes met mine, and I thought I saw an apology in them.

"You left it on the dresser. I sent it back to the rez along with other stuff."

I knew he meant stuff that no longer had any relevance to his life.

"I guess Reid helped himself. I'm sorry, Umlaut."

The apology touched me, and it was a minute before I could speak.

"I left it there because it didn't belong to me anymore." Because you didn't belong to me anymore.

He looked as if he would say more on the subject, but I didn't want to hear anymore.

"Your brother's in big trouble," I said. He nodded. "I've got to talk to him, see if there's any way he can clear himself. Tell me how to get up to the cabin."

His lips twitched. "It takes Reid and me six hours of mostly uphill hiking," he said. "With your wilderness skills, it'd take about three months. You'd have to wait for the snow to melt."

The words were a little harsh, but the tone was mild and teasing, and, in all justice, he was right.

"I'll get a GPS from Max."

His brow furrowed for an instant. "You can't do it," he said, definitively. "Since I want to be present when you grill him, I'll take you up there, but there's one condition: I'll expect you to share any information you gather about the case."

I hesitated on principle. It wasn't that I couldn't trust him or thought he'd take advantage of me. It was just that I resented being asked for a quid pro quo. On the other hand, I knew he was desperately worried about his brother.

"Deal," I said, holding out a hand to shake. He took it in both of his, and for a long moment, he didn't let go. I felt shaken when I finally retrieved it.

"Tomorrow, then," I said, getting up to indicate our meeting was over.

"I'll pick you up before dawn."

I shook my head. "I can't go that early. I've got to help Elli get breakfast for the visiting dignitaries." I told him about the committee from Lansing and the Snow Train. "Pick me up at nine."

"Wear layers. You'll have to strip down to sleep."

"SLEEP?"

He looked surprised at my reaction. "I told you it takes six hours each way. Six and six is twelve. Daylight on the shortest days of the year up here lasts for what, eight hours? Nine? It's too dangerous to hike in the dark. We'll have to stay overnight."

There was a moose sitting on my chest, and I felt the cold sensation behind my nose that always foretells a panic attack. We were going to spend the night together in a remote cabin in the Porkies?

"Chill out, Hatti," he said, in an indifferent voice. "I'm not going to ravish you."

Of course. I sucked in a calming breath. If he'd wanted to ravish me, he'd never have sent me packing twelve months ago.

"Besides, we'll have a chaperone."

There was that, too. Still, spending the night in the mountains seemed uncomfortably intimate for a couple whose next stop was divorce court.

"And, anyway, it might be useful to have that time together. We can tie up our loose ends."

That was what I'd wanted, wasn't it? An explanation of all

that had happened. I wasn't sure I wanted it now. There seemed no point in ripping the scabs off of old wounds.

"I think," I said, rejecting his offer, "we'll just stick to the case."

An hour later I stretched out on my childhood bed and stared up at the glow-in-the-dark stars that Pops and I had stuck to the ceiling half a lifetime ago. What had I been thinking? It had taken me months to put myself back together after the shrapnel blast that ended my marriage, and now I was blithely planning to risk it all by spending a night in the woods with my almost-ex? Had I had any choice? I didn't think so. Not if I wanted to find out what happened to Liisa Pelonen. I realized the curiosity and pride that had impelled me to continue with the case had taken on another, more urgent dimension. Reid Night Wind, on paper and every other way, seemed like the clear winner in the prime suspect sweepstakes, but I found myself rooting against him. I hoped he hadn't killed Liisa, and I hoped we could find evidence supporting that. I knew my hope wasn't rational. Reid already had a police record. But his arrest and conviction would devastate Jace Night Wind, and, in spite of everything, I couldn't bear to have that happen. I continued to stare at the stars and to wonder how this temporary, acting, routine civil servant's job had turned my life upside down.

CHAPTER NINE

The Keweenaw alarm clock woke me again the next morning.

"It is December fifteenth," Betty Ann chirped, "and time for the family trek into the woods to cut down the perfect Christmas tree."

I groaned. Mom and Pops were coming home in four days, if you counted today, and I not only hadn't decorated the house for Christmas, I hadn't cleaned it. I'd have to carve out some time for housekeeping, but first I'd have to survive one night on the mountain.

I threw my legs over the side of the bed and got to my feet. No one had promised life would be easy. I'd created a good, stress-free life for myself during the past year, but I couldn't have expected it to last. I had a responsibility now to the community and to Pops, and I had to meet it. I intended to face the next twenty-four hours with my chin up and my shoulders back. I intended to face it with *sisu*, the indefinable quality of perseverance and courage that Pops was always talking about. And I would.

Right after breakfast.

I dressed in layers of long underwear, flannel-lined jeans, heavy socks, a gray turtleneck and an ancient forest-green sweatshirt that had once belonged to my ex-brother-in-law, Lars, and was imprinted with the mildly clever logo, *Eh, B, C*. I wanted to make it clear to Jace that I was not getting dolled up for him, so I bypassed the makeup, fluffed a brush through my short, spiky hair and applied enough strawberry lip gloss to keep my lips from chapping. Then I fed Larry and set off for the B&B.

I half-expected to get at least an eye roll from Arvo when he spotted my informal attire, but he scarcely glanced at me when I arrived, and he didn't speak to me until after we'd served brunch and cleaned the kitchen, when he pulled me into Elli's powder room for a private conference. Even then he didn't waste time with pleasantries.

In the harsh light of the small room I was able to detect a new spider web of wrinkles crisscrossing his broad forehead. The taut skin of his cheeks and jaw seemed to have sagged overnight. "Pauline and I are taking the guests up to Copper Harbor this morning. It's the last official event of the festival. As soon as they leave town, I intend to call Sheriff Clump."

He seemed braced for opposition from me. I hesitated. Here was an easy way out. All I had to do was turn over the reins to Sheriff Clump. Reid Night Wind would no longer be my responsibility, and his aggravating brother would vanish from my radar screen. I could return to selling bait and knitting needles. I had to admit I was tempted. I gazed at Arvo.

"You said I could have more time."

He shrugged his big shoulders. "Time isn't gonna matter, Hatti-girl," he said. "You can't find out what happened to my Liisa without a proper autopsy." I suddenly remembered what Sonya had discovered, the secret Liisa's surrogate papa didn't know. I knew I should tell him, but as I stared into those kindly, crystal blue eyes, I couldn't bring myself to do it.

"Listen," I said, quickly, "I've got a lead. A good one. Don't call the sheriff yet. Just give me another twenty-four hours."

"You could give the lead to Clump, eh?"

I knew he'd had second thoughts about landing someone so inexperienced with such a big job. Arvo considered himself the godfather to all of Red Jacket.

"This has become important to me," I told him, quietly. "I'm afraid Clump won't bother to find out what really happened to Liisa. I want to know."

"I want to know, too, Hatti-girl," Arvo said, sadly. Abruptly, he smiled. "You are a stubborn Finlander, just like your papa."

I grinned. Carl Lehtinen, who had married my widowed mother when I was a baby, might not be my natural father, but he was my papa, and everyone knew it. Everyone, that is, except Jace Night Wind, who had a kind of complex about it.

"I won't tell Clump. Not yet. You will tell me when you get evidence?"

If there was real, hard, irrefutable evidence. "Yes." I glanced at the visitors from Lansing, laughing and smoking in Elli's smoke-free B&B. It was for them and what they could bring us that we'd hushed up the murder. "What about the Snow Train?"

Arvo gave me two thumbs up. "It's a go."

I nodded. "At least something went right this weekend."

I tried to think through what I needed to do before I met Jace, but I was having trouble focusing. My mind assured me the trek to the mountains was a terrible idea, but the sense of anticipation that had kept me up most of the night had been neither regret nor fear. I wanted to spend the time with Jace, and I knew it was not a good sign.

Sofi and Elli were in the kitchen. I spoke to the former, trying to keep my voice casual.

"Can Charlie take care of the dog overnight?"

"Overnight?" Sofi spoke the word, but both she and my cousin looked at me as if I had two heads. "You're going away overnight?"

I hadn't been away overnight since I'd returned last year.

"I am twenty-eight years old," I pointed out.

"But what about the investigation?" Elli asked.

"I'm trying to track down a clue," I said, wishing they would leave it at that, knowing they wouldn't.

"What clue?" Sofi asked.

I toyed with the idea of a lie but rejected it. I'd never been a smooth liar, and, anyway, my friends knew me too well.

"The dream catcher. Reid Night Wind gave the necklace to Liisa. I'm going to talk to him."

Sofi paled and put a hand on her chest. "You're going out to the rez?"

It was so much worse than that.

I shook my head. "Reid's camped out in a cabin. I'm going to talk to him there."

"It's too dangerous," Elli protested. "What if Reid Night Wind's the killer?"

I almost smiled. During all the hours I'd spent worrying about the danger involved in this outing, I'd never once thought my life was threatened. As I looked at those two worried faces, I knew I was going to have to be more specific.

"The cabin's up in the mountains. I'm going with Jace. I'll be fine."

Sofi's eyes narrowed. I could hear the bitterness in her voice.

"Don't be a fool, Hatti. Don't get mixed up with that guy again. He's bad news."

I couldn't blame her. There hadn't been time for my family to meet my husband, and all they knew was that he'd rejected me after six months.

"This is just business." I spoke crisply and, I hoped, re-assuringly. "I need to talk to Reid. Jace knows how to find him. I'll be back tomorrow in one piece, I promise you."

"I'll come with you," Elli said, suddenly.

I grinned at my pixie of a cousin.

"I can handle this, El. You'll see. Why don't you call an emergency meeting of the knitting circle for tomorrow night?

You all see what you can sniff out around town, and I'll fill you in on what I've learned. Deal? Now, can someone take care of the dog?"

Jace was lounging against the railing on my parents' front porch like a lean, hungry jungle cat who'd strayed too far north. I felt that annoying bump in my heartbeat that was all too reminiscent of our courtship and marriage. I reminded myself that he was descended from a shaman, which probably accounted for the magic. Was there any way to break the spell? Time, probably. Time was pretty much the cure for everything.

He looked at me oddly. There had been a time he'd have said, "You look philosophical." Not today.

"We'll take the pickup," he said, sticking to business. I nodded and almost thanked him. When he spoke again, though, I heard the challenge in his voice and knew he was establishing the ground rules. He was in charge of this expedition. I wasn't getting into an argument over that.

"Fine. Just let me get my backpack."

I hadn't heard him follow me inside, but when I returned to the door he was down on his haunches rubbing Larry's ears.

"Did you make arrangements for the dog?"

My eyes narrowed on him. "There's no need. Larry likes to have the house to himself. He'll probably do a colon cleanse, take a sauna and meditate."

Jace smiled, and my heart jumped. It was the first time I'd seen him smile in more than a year. I'd forgotten its effect on me.

"Sorry."

"No sweat. Want to sign the divorce papers while you're here?"

"Nah. I'll want an attorney to look them over."

"You are an attorney."

"We're already late, Hatti. I'd like to get there before dusk."

"Fine," I said, a little tired of agreeing to everything. "You can sign them tomorrow."

The truck was an old one, a white, battered pickup that I suspected belonged to Chief Joseph and was not the car Jace had driven to the U.P. I scanned the horizon as he turned the pickup around, drove down Calumet to Tamarack Street, then hopped onto M-41 going west.

"Coast clear?"

I heard the sarcasm in his voice and wondered at it.

"What're you talking about?"

"You seem jumpy, like you don't want any of your friends to see you with me."

"My friends know about this outing," I said. "And I'm not jumpy. Just anxious to get some answers on the case. And I don't want to raise suspicion. Liisa's death isn't common knowledge yet."

"Don't be ridiculous. You, of all people, know about small town grapevines. There are no secrets in a closed community like this one. I doubt if there's anybody under the age of ninety or over the age of four who doesn't know about this."

I stared at him. "Was that what it was like on the rez? Everybody knew your business?"

"Every last sordid detail."

I could only imagine how painful that must have been, but I was pretty sure he didn't want my sympathy.

"It doesn't matter anymore," I said. "The festival's over in a couple of hours. Arvo told me this morning he was going to turn it over to the sheriff. I asked for a little more time, but I'm not sure even Arvo can control this thing."

Jace nodded grimly, his eyes on the road ahead. "Clump's not gonna like being left out of the loop."

"He'll be all right with it if I can hand him a suspect on a silver platter."

"You mean Reid?"

I heard the hoarseness under the words. So he wasn't certain about his brother's innocence. Dang.

"We don't know that yet."

"It's not Reid."

"If you're so sure, why're you wasting time taking me up the mountain?"

He had to keep his eyes on the slick road, but I caught a flash of his old smile.

"If you have to ask me that, you've really changed."

Fury boiled up inside me.

"Pull over."

"What?" He glanced at me.

"Pull. Over. I want to turn around."

"What're you talking about?"

"All I have to do is tell Sheriff Clump where your brother's hiding, Jace. I don't have to go up there."

He was silent a moment. "What did I say?"

"Don't you know? You were flirting with me."

There was another short pause.

"Sorry," he said, briefly. "It's just habit."

I considered pointing out that he'd broken the habit twelve months earlier, that if he'd been flirting lately it wasn't with me, but I didn't really want to get into a personal conversation. I just wanted to find out what had happened to Liisa Pelonen.

"Anything between us," I reminded him, "is strictly business. By your choice."

He kept his eyes on the road.

"One last personal remark. What did you do with the dream catcher?"

"I have it."

"I want you to keep it."

I shook my head. "It's evidence at the moment. When this is over you—or Reid—can have it back."

"I gave it to you."

"Save it for your next wife."

I sounded bitter, and I found myself feeling grateful that he didn't point that out. Strictly business, I reminded myself as he drove through the falling snow and I gazed out the window.

"What about the father?" Jace asked, moving away from the quicksand of our failed relationship. "Does he know about the girl's death?"

I explained about the ice fishing.

"Could he have killed her?"

I'd thought about that, too. "I suppose he could have, but why would he? He was her father."

"It wouldn't be the first time."

"There's no reason, though. She'd moved out. She wasn't costing him any money. She was nearly grown up. I'm sure there was a bond between them."

"Why?"

I frowned at him. "Don't be so cynical."

"I'm not. I'm looking for suspects. Most murders are domestic. Pelonen and the girl had no other relatives, right? He's a natural suspect."

"Only if he's insane."

"People kill for lots of reasons but mainly greed. They're not all insane."

"Liisa was a sweet, lovely, beautiful girl," I said, with more conviction than I felt. "And there was no money. Greed was not the motive."

"Maybe he killed her because she'd gotten pregnant."

It wasn't entirely implausible on the face of it, but it was unlikely. Unwed pregnancy wasn't encouraged in our community, but it wasn't considered a disaster, either, probably because it happened with some regularity. There just wasn't all that much for kids to do during the winter time.

"He wouldn't have killed her for that," I said, positively, "and, anyway, he probably didn't know about it. It was only six weeks."

My almost ex-husband took his eyes off the road long enough to shoot me a look of astonishment.

"There are tests now that report accurately within a couple of days."

"And you'd have reason to know?"

"Anyone could know. And, yes, I've gotten involved with some paternity cases." He paused. "What about Arvo Maki?"

I gaped at him. "Are you suggesting Arvo killed her because she got pregnant?"

"Maybe it was his baby."

I shook my head. "You might just as well suggest it was Reverend Sorensen's baby or Pops's. I know these guys, Jace. That baby was fathered by one of two people, Matti Murso or your brother."

"You can't know that."

"How is that different from you claiming that Reid isn't the murderer?"

"What happens if we turn up strong evidence in favor of one of these older guys?"

I shook my head. "In the case of Arvo, I'd accept nothing less than a confession. Besides, I have his wife's word that he didn't even know about it. He still doesn't."

"Tell me more about Matti Murso."

"He's seventeen, a hockey star and, until Liisa Pelonen came to town, he'd been planning to marry the pharmacist's daughter."

"Hell hath no fury?"

I laughed and relaxed a little. "I thought that might apply to

Ronja Laplander, the woman who was so angry at Arvo for choosing Liisa as this year's St. Lucy."

"Missing out on St. Lucy doesn't compare with a broken engagement."

"You don't understand this community. Getting picked as St. Lucy is like getting an Academy Award. It sets a girl up for life. At least that's what the mamas believe."

He cursed, softly. "How can you stand living in this place? All these people do is make mountains out of molehills."

"Priorities might look different, but they aren't, really. People are driven by a need to succeed, to provide support for their families, to keep them and the community strong."

"Where does murder come into it?"

"I think murder happens when something destroys the things that are important."

"Or when there's an opportunity to add to the coffers."

I smiled, ruefully. "Have you always been this cynical?"

"Probably."

"You know, you remind me of Lars."

"Who the hell's Lars?"

I barely heard him as inspiration struck me. I dug my cellphone out of my backpack and punched in a number.

"Hey, Squirt."

"Hey. I need a big favor."

"You got it." It was one of the many qualities I'd always loved about my brother-in-law. There was no muss, no fuss, no equivocating. Just support and love and good judgment. Except the time three years ago when he'd spent the night with a barmaid at the Black Fly.

"Jalmer Pelonen's out on Lake Gogebic ice fishing. I need someone to find him."

"Okay."

"Lars? I want to tell you why. Jalmer's daughter, Liisa, the one who was living with Arvo and Pauline Maki, was killed Friday night. It may have been murder."

He whistled. "Hell."

"Yep."

"I'll get back to you."

I hung up and Jace glanced at me.

"Squirt?"

"Lars is my sister's ex," I said, marveling at how little we knew about each other's families. "They married in high school and lived with us for years. He's not my brother-in-law anymore, but he's still my brother. And he's a private investigator."

"Why'd they get divorced?"

I hesitated. "It sounds worse than it really was."

"Infidelity?"

I made a face. "How'd you know?"

"Educated guess."

"Things were hard. They'd been married a long time and parents nearly as long. They never went to college, and it got harder and harder to find a good job."

"Let me guess. Waitress? Bartender?"

"It was just one night."

"Not much consolation for your sister."

I shook my head. Sofi had never been able to get over it. I wasn't sure she had even tried.

"My niece misses her dad."

"You're in favor of forgiveness?"

I shrugged. "He's sorry. He had too much to drink. He's on the wagon now."

He didn't respond to that, and I figured he'd gotten bored. Marriage, after all, was hardly his favorite subject.

The pickup ate up the miles despite the worsening conditions of the roads. Soon I saw the Quincy Mine's shaft rise up out of the ground, and I knew we were just north of Hancock. The city is built on a hillside, and we zigged and zagged as M-26 led us past weatherworn houses, then onto Quincy Street past Finlandia University, Humalalampi's Flowers, Rissanen's Jewelers and Ryti's Market. The ethnic influence is so pervasive in Hancock that each street sign carries both an English and a Finnish name, and every winter the city hosts *Heikinpaiva,* a festival to celebrate the feast day of Finland's patron saint, St. Heinrik, for whom I am named.

We stayed on M-26 as we crossed the Portage Lake Bridge that spans the Keweenaw Waterway and connects Copper County with the more prosperous lower half. Houghton, Hancock's sister city, is the home of Michigan Technological University, and usually there are students thronging the streets. Not today though. It was Christmas break.

Jace's windshield wipers fought to clear the snow that fell more and more heavily as we headed south through the countryside. Our world felt insular and, thanks to the pickup's heater, toasty warm. I must have started to doze, because his next words seemed like something out of a dream.

"Did you know that the Ojibwe have a creation legend like your Kalevala?"

I stared at him, shocked that he knew of the Kalevala. He'd never shown any interest in Finnish lore, or in Ojibwe legend, for that matter. He didn't wait for me to answer.

"It's the story of Waynaboozhoo, the original man, who was both a human and a spirit."

"Kind of like Jesus."

"Hmmm." Jace kept his eyes on the slick pavement. Visibility was decreasing fast, but he drove with confidence, the same way he did everything else.

"The Creator, Gitchee Manitou, told Waynaboozoo to go all over the earth and name everything he saw, plants and animals and bodies of water, the seasons, the sun, moon and stars."

"Big job."

He glanced at me but continued the story. "In his travels, Waynaboozoo met his mother, the earth, his grandmother, the moon, his father, the sun and his uncle, the wind."

A well-connected guy. This time I kept the thought to myself. Why was he telling me this? What was going on here?

"One day Waynaboozoo learned that he had a twin brother. He set out to find his twin, but he didn't know where to look. A spirit guide, Bugwayjinini, appeared to help him out."

Jace's voice shifted from a narrative singsong to a slow, rhythmic monologue. I could imagine him sitting cross-legged in front of a campfire, holding the other members of the tribe spellbound with his story.

" 'Your shadow brother is your other side,' Bugwayjinini told Waynaboozhoo. 'There are differences between you. You will walk the path of peace, while he would not. You are kind, while he is not. You are humble and generous. He is not. You seek the good in others, but he does not. You are the light, Waynaboozhoo. He is the darkness. Know that your brother is with you. Understand him but do not seek him.' "

I felt tears prick the backs of my eyes as Jace became once again the man I'd fallen in love with. I understood the story. I understood the message. He wanted me to know that he, like Waynaboozhoo and every other person who has walked the earth, had a dark side. Was this his way of accepting the responsibility for what had happened between us? Would he tell me the rest of it? I knew I couldn't ask him. I knew the specifics would have to come in his own time. When I understood it all, would I be able to forgive him? Was that what he wanted? The questions ricocheted in my head, but I came up with no answers.

We continued the trip in silence, eventually turning onto an unmarked road that, almost immediately, slanted upward at a nearly forty-five-degree angle. I recognized the area, having been here before in the summer. After a short drive we turned off on the dirt road that led to Silver City and Lake of the Clouds, a pristine body of water located between two ridges of the Porcupine Mountain Range. The lake's name came from the placid surface that reflected the sky.

Another hour brought us to the end of an old logging road, where we found an ancient, rusty pickup truck covered in several inches of snow.

"Reid's?"

Jace nodded. We parked and slung our arms into our backpacks. Jace carried the larger one, and loaded on top were not one, but two, sleeping bags. I frowned.

"I can carry my own."

His smile was slow and teasing, and it did unfortunate things to my insides.

"I'd rather carry two sleeping bags now than have to carry you, too, when you finally collapse."

"I'm not going to collapse," I snapped.

"Don't be so prickly. You're not exactly a Campfire Girl. You had to be bribed to take a walk on the C and O canal path by the Potomac River."

I didn't appreciate the walks down Bad Memory Lane. "Maybe I've changed now that I'm back in the north woods. This is my home, remember?"

"I remember lots of things," he said, and I was pretty sure he was still talking about our marriage. I considered issuing another reprimand, but he went silent as his gaze traveled down my form until it reached my feet. He frowned. "Where the hell did you get those boots?"

"Aren't they great? They're Zamberlan Three-tens, the Jimmy Choo's of hiking boots," I said. "I got them from Max."

"That damned cowboy?"

"Ex-cowboy. Now he's a fish boy. He bought *Namagok,* the

old fishing camp, and he stocks outdoor gear for his guests. He gave me a discount on the boots." Jace's scowl startled me. "He did the same for Sofi and Elli. Not that it's any of your business. Sofi and Elli are my sister and my . . ."

"I know who they are," he growled. "Let's go."

He started toward the path that was undoubtedly buried under the half a foot of snow, and I trotted along behind him in my brand new, luxury boots.

It was a long, hard slog. Not only did we have bits of hail the size of baby peas pinging against our faces, but the path was narrow and mostly uphill. Some of the trail was bare, but more often we ran into drifts, and negotiating them was like trying to wade through oatmeal. Fallen branches hidden under the snow presented additional hazards, as did patches of camouflaged ice.

After two hours we reached a treeless plateau where we paused out of deference to my heavy breathing and beet-red face. Jace, of course, looked as fresh as a mountain goat. He extracted two bottles of water from his pack, and, even though I had my own, it was easier to just accept the one he handed me. I chugged, my hand shaking with fatigue.

"Not so fast," he murmured. "You'll get cramps."

I slowed down. After all, he was the one with woods experience. When I finished, I looked around.

"This is a tailing field." I'd spent some time last winter reading books about the local area, books I found in Pops's study. I figured the history of the Finnish copper miners represented a desirable contrast to Washington, D.C., and the life I had just left. I didn't expect Jace to show a particle of interest in the subject, but he surprised me.

"The field was used for dumping poor rock after the copper was extracted from it," he said. "The rocks lying here have been in place for seventy years. I know where most of 'em are because Grandfather, Reid and I made this trip dozens of times when we were building the cabin. If you don't want to break an ankle, you'd better take my hand."

He didn't wait for me to weigh the pros and cons of the suggestion. He just scooped my mittened hand into his, and I let him. I didn't want to break an ankle or anything else, and, after a few minutes, the strength that flowed through his arm to me seemed to help me recover my breath, but I kept my mouth shut. It was hard enough to manage the hike and the unnerving proximity to my sexy ex. I needed to hoard my oxygen and my thoughts.

The next break occurred two hours later. This time I drank my own water, but I did it slowly while I closed my eyes and leaned against a solid tree trunk and wished I could just slide down onto the soft-looking snow.

"How'd you get saddled with this job?"

"What?" I kept my eyes closed.

"Police chief. Surely there was somebody in town with better qualifications."

I decided not to take offense. It was, after all, a legitimate point. I shrugged, reveling in the relief of not having that pack on my shoulders.

"Most folks in the U.P. wear more than one hat. Arvo asked me to do it after my dad got hurt in a snowmobile accident."

"Your stepdad."

I opened one eye, but I was too weary to argue. "He's the only dad I've ever known. Or ever needed. How much farther to the cabin?"

"You'll be relieved to know it's around the corner. Two hundred yards. I warn you, it's pretty primitive."

I laughed. "Relieved is the right word. If it's got indoor plumbing, I'll consider it Xanadu."

We started to walk, and, an instant later, I saw a small, square structure built against a hillside and buffered with pines. It looked as solid and dependable as a good marriage.

A harsh expletive exploded from Jace's mouth, and I gazed at him, startled. "What's wrong?"

"There's no smoke from the chimney. Reid's not here."

Chapter Ten

"Are you saying we'll be spending the night alone?"

"You, me and a couple of sandwiches. Unless, of course, you want to hike back down the mountain in the dark."

Anger flared. "You promised me I'd get to speak to him. You said he'd be up here."

The look on Jace's face was almost savage.

"You think this is a plan to get you alone? Believe me, Umlaut. I'm not that much of a fool."

His use of the nickname should have enraged me. Instead, it calmed me down. He hadn't planned this. He'd thought Reid would be here.

"Maybe there's a note inside," he said, in a calmer voice.

"Yeah. Or a written confession."

"Sarcasm doesn't become you, Hatti." He opened the unlocked door.

The single room was small and cold, but there was a tumble of bedding in one corner, indicating recent habitation. Jace nodded at a door on one side of the room. "That's the head."

I was so relieved to discover there *was* a head that for a moment I forgot the cold, the bone-wearying fatigue and my irritation at the company. Jace set about building a fire, and the dancing flames lifted my mood even more. There had been a time when I'd have reveled in the prospect of a night alone with Jace Night Wind in a remote cabin or on the moon or anywhere else, and, perhaps unfortunately, I could still recall the feeling.

While Jace melted snow over the fire in preparation for making coffee, I unwrapped the food, which included ham-and-cheese hoagies provided by Jace, and stale, raisin-studded granola bars provided by me. When the coffee was ready, we sat cross-legged to eat in front of the fire.

"Nothing," I said, after I'd inhaled the sandwich, "has ever tasted this good."

"Mountain climbing builds one hell of an appetite," he said, with a low chuckle. "Which you would already know if we'd made it past the first two hundred yards that time we decided to hike the Appalachian Trail."

"I would have done better in these boots," I said. He gave me a penetrating look. "Or, if we hadn't run into a snake."

He shook his head. "With your, er, aversion to everything that crawls, how have you ended up running a bait shop?"

"I try not to think too much about what's in the refrigerator. And I've got Einar. He handles the live bait and, well, pretty much everything else related to fishing. I mostly focus on yarn and knitting supplies."

"Einar?"

I grinned, thinking of the old man. "He's a tonttu. I mean, he looks like one. Short, bald, with the bluest eyes you've ever seen. He hardly ever talks back; well," I amended, "he hardly ever talks at all. The only thing that will bring out the words is his distress over our husband-less situation—Sofi's and mine."

"You aren't husbandless."

His unequivocal and unexpected response ripped through the fragile sense of détente we'd enjoyed. There was too much bitterness and mistrust between us. We couldn't be companionable. Former lovers were, I thought, further apart than people who'd never even met. Those people still had a chance to meet and connect. We had no chance at all.

I hid the wave of sadness that washed over me. There was no

point in raking over old bones.

"So what's up between you and Max? You want to date him? That why you want a quickie divorce?"

"It's hardly a quickie divorce. We've been separated for twelve months."

"That's not an answer."

"What makes you think you deserve an answer, Jace? This separation was all your doing. All of it. Who I date and when is not your business."

"It is until the divorce is final." I scowled at him. "So, what's the verdict? Do you want to date him?"

I knew, in that moment, that I didn't. I liked Max. We were friends. Why ruin a good friendship by loading it up with baggage, like sex and emotions?

"I haven't decided," I said. "We've got some things in common."

"Like what? Fishing?"

"Yep. I run a bait shop, remember?"

"How'd you get into that, anyway?"

"I needed a job." And I needed an occupation to help me regain my sanity. "Pops turned over the shop to me. I'm buying it from him on the installment plan."

For once he didn't mention the word "stepdad."

"We have something else in common, too. Max is a newcomer, and I've recently returned. We have a certain amount of perspective that the rest of my family lacks, and, at the same time, we value our home because we've made conscious decisions to live there."

"You 'valued your home' in D.C."

I wasn't sure that was true. I'd been happy because I'd been with him.

"That was then. This is where I belong now."

He rose to punch up the fire, then returned without saying

anything. I thought about how odd it was that I felt comfortable with him and figured that comfort must be like muscle memory. Once the impression is imprinted, the feeling lingers. But it was a fragile feeling, easily torn to shreds as soon as one of us opened our mouth.

"Just so you know, I haven't dated anyone."

"Not even that hot new girl in the office? Natasha what's her name?"

He held out his left hand to show me he was still wearing the thin band of white gold.

"What're you waiting for?"

He shrugged. "I still feel married." *I've missed you.* He didn't complete the thought aloud, but I heard it anyway, and a lump formed in my throat. How was I supposed to respond to that? The dissolution of the marriage had been all his idea.

"I'm sorry," he said. "I'm sorry I never explained."

Not, I noted, sorry he'd dumped me.

"It was for the best," I said, briskly, getting to my feet to clean up the meal. "I'm back where I belong."

Sometimes I even believed that.

"Tell me about St. Lucy," he said, later, after we'd settled into our sleeping bags for the night. "You played her at one time, didn't you?"

I was surprised he knew about that. I must have droned on about the experience during one of our marathon talk sessions in the weeks before we married.

"St. Lucy's kind of an aberration for Finns. As a rule, Lutherans don't have a lot of truck, as my mom would say, with saints, but St. Lucy is different. She was supposedly an early Christian who refused an offer of marriage from an Italian nobleman because she wanted to remain pure for Jesus. The nobleman's cronies made her into a martyr by killing her with a sword thrust to one eye. She's celebrated in Scandinavian countries more as a symbol of light during a season of darkness. She wears a white robe with a blood-red sash and an evergreen crown of candles on her head." I shrugged. "It's an honor to be chosen, and there's a sort of unofficial belief that a season of playing St. Lucy sets a girl up for a good marriage and a good life."

"It didn't work for Liisa Pelonen."

"It's just a myth. There was a lot of flap about it this year because Arvo bypassed protocol and chose the St. Lucy by himself. One woman in particular, Astrid Laplander, was furious. She maintained it was her daughter's turn to play the role. She complained to me every day for a week." I paused. "Did Reid tell your grandfather what Liisa was wearing when he found her?"

Jace's grunt meant he didn't know.

"It was her costume. The weird thing was that she'd taken it off an hour before, had a shower and a cup of tea and gone to bed in her nightgown, with a dose of Vicks VapoRub to cure her scratchy throat. No one seems to know why she got up and put on the costume."

"Sounds wacky," Jace said. "Maybe Reid will have the answer."

"I hope so." I hoped, too, that Reid would put in an appearance soon. This set-up was entirely too cozy.

My soon-to-be-ex husband must have been restless, too, because he sat up and ran his fingers through his hair.

"Let's go over what we know. You first."

I thought it was a good idea. It seemed to me that trying to solve a crime was like trying to put together a puzzle, only first you had to find the pieces. We needed more pieces, and we needed to see which spaces were still empty.

"I'll start with the parade. Not surprisingly, Liisa caught a chill riding down Main Street wearing only the white cotton robe, and she complained of a sore throat."

"Stop. How do you know that?"

"Because I was St. Lucy, and I remember how cold it was. And because Pauline told me."

"Continue."

"Pauline whisked her back to the house, sent her to the shower, then bundled her into her flannel nightgown—the one with the rosebuds, if you want the details—gave her a cup of tea laced with honey and tucked her into bed, after rubbing her chest with Vicks."

"The details are important, Hatti. Sometimes they make all the difference. What time did all that happen?"

"Pauline said they got home a little before six and that Liisa was in bed by six thirty. Pauline then came over to smorgasbord."

"So no one saw her again until the Makis returned home at nine?"

"You mean other than Reid? Pauline saw her again. She scooted back home around six forty-five to pick up some jars of jam—cloudberry—for the visitors, and she peeked into Liisa's room, found the girl asleep and returned to the B&B."

"So all of this comes from Mrs. Maki."

"Of course. She was the one taking care of Liisa." I eyed him in the semi-darkness. "Surely you're not considering Pauline Maki as the murderer."

"Why not?"

"Well, for one thing, she loved Liisa. I saw her grief on Friday night. And I saw the way Pauline decorated the room for the girl and all the things she bought her."

"Some of that was before Liisa got there, right? Pauline might have gotten tired of having a semi-permanent houseguest."

I shook my head. "You don't understand our culture, Jace. People in Red Jacket take care of each other. It was natural for

Pauline and Arvo to offer Liisa a home for a year. It would be natural for any of us."

"I defer to your greater knowledge of the community."

"Thank you. And there's something else. I can't help thinking Liisa's baby is at the core of this. And I'm one hundred percent sure Pauline didn't make Liisa pregnant."

He said nothing, possibly because he didn't agree with me or maybe because the baby motive would fit his brother.

"Tell me what happened when the Makis found her."

"When they realized she wasn't in her bed, they searched the house, the greenhouse and finally the sauna."

"Why the sauna last?"

"Arvo said Liisa didn't use it much. Apparently she'd had enough saunas in her dad's cabin in Ahmeek." He nodded.

"Anyway, she was sprawled on the floor with a cut on her head."

"Where was the nightgown?"

I stared at him. "I don't know. Wait. Yes, I do! It was in Liisa's drawer. I saw it when I searched her room."

He stared back at me. "Why would she have taken off her nightgown and changed back into her costume?"

"That's the big question. The robe is comfortable enough, but the crown has to be wired into the hair. It would have been difficult, if not impossible, to do alone. It just doesn't make sense."

Jace frowned into the glowing embers of the fire.

"Reid was supposed to meet her at seven P.M., but he was a few minutes late. His guess was five or ten minutes, which means it was more like twenty or thirty. He let himself into the sauna with a key she'd given him, and there she was on the floor."

"So between the time Pauline left her at six forty-five and, say, seven thirty at the latest, she got up, changed from her nightie to her costume, went down to the sauna to wait for Reid and somebody killed her. You've got to admit it doesn't look good for Reid."

"He has no motive, Hatti."

"What about the baby?"

"We don't know that it was his, but even if it was, there was no reason to kill the girl."

"What about child support?"

Jace shook his head. "He couldn't have done it." His voice was more tentative, though, as if he were trying to convince himself. "He wouldn't have hit her with a rock."

"Sonya believes the blow happened either just before or just after the death, but that it wasn't hard enough to kill her. We'll have to wait for the official autopsy to find out the real cause of death." I paused. "I'm starting to think she was poisoned, Jace, and hit on the head to divert attention from that possibility."

"Imaginative."

"Poison should show up on an autopsy screening, shouldn't it?" He nodded. I wondered if he was thinking about Reid's experience with drugs in the cat lab.

"Where was Maki during the hour between six forty-five and seven forty-five?"

"At the Leaping Deer with the guests from Lansing."

"Every moment?"

"I don't know. I didn't have a tracker device on him."

"Pity. What about the other suspects?"

"You mean Diane Hakala and Ronja Laplander? They left the smorgasbord right after dinner to chaperone the Snowflake Dance."

"What about the hockey player?"

"I don't know. He didn't attend the dance."

"And the Hakala girl?"

"She didn't attend it, either."

"Maybe they did it together. Maybe all of them did it together."

"A la 'Murder on the Orient Express'?"

I shook my head, wearily. I couldn't believe that Diane, Ronja, Barb or Matti had killed Liisa Pelonen. I couldn't believe Arvo had, either. That left Reid Night Wind.

"We need more information," I said, finally. "In the meantime, I'm going to sleep."

"Dream about this: Half the town was at the smorgasbord, less than a hundred feet away from the murder scene. Practically anyone in Red Jacket could have committed the murder."

Not, I thought, as I closed my eyes, an uplifting thought.

Ignatius Holomo, Red Jacket's oldest living inhabitant for as long as I could remember, had finally given up his title and was, as Pops put it, "heading to the marble orchard."

I walked over to Makis' with my parents and Sofi to pay my respects. Everyone in town was there, too, queued up to file past the coffin while Miss Irene played Sibelius's "Be Still My Soul" on the Makis' upright, the way she does for all our funerals. The scent of roses was strong, and I felt the familiar discomfort. I am not a fan of funerals in general, and my least favorite part is the "viewing of the body." As a child, I'd developed the trick of focusing on a corner of the raised coffin lid, thereby avoiding a face-to-face with the deceased. But now I was an adult, and conscience interfered. I forced my gaze to Ignatius's grizzled face, intending to offer him a silent "R.I.P.," but the silence was broken by a series of short, sharp shrieks. It took a minute to realize they were coming from me. My heart slammed against my ribs so hard that it hurt, and I couldn't seem to catch my breath. And then I woke. There was a suffocating weight on my chest and a gentle voice in my ear.

"You're all right, honey. It was just a bad dream."

Jace's voice. For a moment I was confused again. Was I awake, or was this a dream? Had the nightmare of my separation been a dream, or had it been real? I struggled with the question just as I struggled to get enough air. And then the weight lifted, but I could feel his heat hovering above my body, and I could feel his fingers on my face.

"Dreaming about the murder?"

"I was at a funeral," I said, remembering the countless times I'd bored him with a recitation of my dreams. "Ignatius Holomo finally died. But when I looked into the coffin, it was you."

He chuckled almost silently.

"That was probably just wishful thinking."

His fingers drew a line down my cheek, and then I felt his lips against mine. It was a chaste kiss, sweet and comforting, and I wanted to cry. That impulse, thank goodness, was checked when the cabin door opened, letting in a blast of snow and cold, and a powerful flashlight made me shut my eyes. I heard Jace's curse and felt his withdrawal as the newcomer spoke.

"Well, damn, big brother. I thought you'd come up here to rescue me."

CHAPTER ELEVEN

Embarrassed and annoyed because I'd been caught in a compromising position, and because I had to meet my prime suspect for the first time under such disadvantageous circumstances, I struggled to my feet.

"Don't get up on my account," said Reid Night Wind. He'd set the flashlight on its end so it illuminated the room, and I got my first glimpse of my brother-in-law. I was not surprised to discover he was as devastatingly attractive as Jace. More so. His long hair was tied back, emphasizing cheekbones that could have cut a steak. His nose was straight, his chin strong and his features arranged symmetrically. He was slightly shorter than his brother and even more slender. His teeth flashed white in the shadowed room. I was well aware of my disheveled clothing and the hair that undoubtedly looked as if it had been attacked with an eggbeater. I resisted the urge to smooth it and held out my hand.

"I'm Hatti Lehtinen."

"I'm relieved to hear it," Reid said, taking my hand and raising it to his lips. "I'd hate to find my brother on top of someone else's wife."

Smooth, I thought. Too smooth for someone who was not yet twenty-two. I thought he might be capable of planning and executing a crime, and the thought saddened me.

"I'm glad you dropped by. I've got some questions."

Reid nodded. "Grandfather said you were Red Jacket's top cop."

"Temporary top cop."

"Temporary, acting," Jace put in. I thought I heard an edge in his voice. "Temporary job, temporary husband. Temporary is a popular concept with Hatti these days."

When we gathered, cross-legged, on the floor, I got a better look at Reid's face. His eyes were not gray like Jace's. They were dark, and in them I could read the anxiety he concealed with his breezy manner. This young man knew he was in trouble.

"What do you want to know?"

I opened my mouth to ask for his timetable of the fatal night, but something else came out.

"Did you kill Liisa Pelonen?" Jace's lips tightened, but he said nothing.

"No. Next question."

"Do you know who did kill her?"

"No, again."

"You'd arranged to meet her Friday night at the sauna?"

"That's right, but I was late."

"How late?"

The younger man looked at his brother. "I don't know. I'm always late."

"How did you get into the sauna?" The question came from Jace.

"I had a key that Liisa had given me, but I didn't need it. Nobody locks up much in Red Jacket."

"So I've noticed," Jace said, with a sideways glance at me.

We ran through the standard questions, and his answers tallied with what we already knew. He had planned to take Liisa to Marquette that night. She'd told him she never wanted to come back to Red Jacket. She had not told him why.

"Where you surprised to find her in the St. Lucy costume?"

Reid shrugged. "I never thought about that. I felt for a pulse, and when I couldn't find it I couldn't think of anything except getting out of there. I knew I'd be blamed."

"So you felt nothing? Not even grief?"

"Later. Not grief, exactly, but I was sorry for the kid. She'd gotten herself into a helluva mess."

"Were you in love with her?"

"No. We were friends."

"You were just friends, and yet you gave her a family heirloom."

He looked uncomfortable. "Yeah, I gave it to her. I thought it was pretty."

I'd thought it was pretty, too. I continued with the questions.

"So, as a friend, you decided to help her run away. That was very altruistic."

He looked into the fire, and I got the impression he was embarrassed.

"Not really. There was money involved. She was gonna pay me."

I knew Jace's groan was inaudible, but I heard it anyway.

"Can you explain that?"

"It's a long story."

I nodded. "We have all night."

"All right. I met Liisa last fall." He glanced from the fire to me, then back again. "I met her at your house. Your dad introduced us."

"Her stepdad," Jace snapped. Both Reid and I ignored him.

"Go on."

"I'd gotten to know Carl after he stopped me for speeding. He coulda given me a ticket. Instead he invited me over to play pool."

That sounded like Pops. He'd have saved every kid in the world if it had been possible.

"How often were you at the house? I never saw you."

"I came over on Thursdays."

"Of course." I turned to Jace. "Thursday is knitting circle night at my shop, and my mom plays bingo at St. Heikki's. Pops has the house to himself." Jace responded with a grunt.

"One night," Reid went on, "the funeral director came over. He brought Liisa with him, and we got talking."

I had no trouble imagining the scene. Both Reid and Liisa were extraordinarily good looking people. The chemistry must have sizzled, and yet, he'd said he and Liisa were just friends.

"It wasn't love at first sight?"

Reid chuckled. "She was a knock-out and should've been just my type. I never felt that way about her though. She seemed like she was in trouble, and I felt sorry for her."

My pulse jumped. "What kind of trouble?"

"She wouldn't tell me. Not at first. But I gave her my cell number, and she started to call me. She said she was scared of 'things.' Things changed in November when she found out she was pregnant. She wanted to go away."

"Was it because she was ashamed?"

"Not exactly. I mean, the baby wasn't planned, but I don't think she was afraid of being shunned or anything." I glanced at Jace as if to say, See? I told you it wouldn't be a deal-breaker in our town.

"She felt like she was in danger, though. She asked me to marry her and take her away, and so I did."

There was a shocked silence while Jace and I tried to absorb this startling remark. Finally, I spoke.

"You didn't love her, but you married her just because she asked?"

He shrugged. "I grew up with a single mom." He looked at Jace. "I knew what it was like."

"Was it your baby?"

Reid's eyes narrowed on his brother's face. "No. Not that I expect you to believe that."

I was still struggling to understand. "Couldn't you have taken her away and even stayed with her without marrying her?"

The laughter had gone out of the dark eyes when they turned to me.

"That's where the money comes in. There was a trust fund— two million dollars—left to Liisa by her mother. The trust stipulated she could have the money when she was twenty-one or, if she married earlier than that, any time after eighteen."

"She turned eighteen on Friday." I gasped. Reid nodded.

"She cut out on the St. Lucy thing, and we drove down to l'Anse and got hitched."

"Geez Louise." I glanced at Jace. There was a money motive, after all.

"Who knew about the trust fund?" Jace asked.

"Her dad, I guess. I don't know. She was gonna take the marriage license to the lawyers on Monday."

"And then what?"

Reid looked at his brother. "Huh?"

"Was she planning to split it with you? A million each and, after a quickie divorce, you'd go your separate ways?"

Reid's mouth twisted into an ugly expression.

"You're close. She did promise me some money. Ten thousand. And we agreed to stay married as long as necessary to make sure the rest of the money was absolutely hers."

Disgust was written all over my husband's dark face. He was disappointed in Reid's bargain, and I thought he was probably blaming himself. I knew he'd assumed responsibility for the younger man years earlier and that he felt guilty for leaving the child with his grandfather.

"She wanted the money, and she didn't want to wait three years. It was convenient for her to have a husband with a baby on the way."

"And it was convenient for you to get a financial windfall," Jace bit out.

"Yeah." Reid didn't sound proud, but he didn't sound apologetic, either. He'd done what he'd done, and he didn't try to excuse himself.

"Who," Jace said, staring at his brother, "inherits the rest of the two million now that Liisa's dead?"

I couldn't tell whether the color drained from Reid's face, but the bones in his face became more pronounced, his cheeks more hollow. I could tell that Jace's point hadn't occurred to him before, but that he had immediately understood the implications.

"I hope to hell it isn't me," he said.

I glanced at Jace. He'd been shocked and horrified by the revelation about the trust fund but not about Reid's revelation of the marriage.

"You knew," I said, accusingly. "You knew they'd gotten married Friday morning." Anguish made my voice louder than intended. "I told you everything I knew, and you withheld the most important fact of all. So much for our pact of transparency."

I didn't need Jace's frown to remind me that I'd chosen the wrong time and place for the argument. I was supposed to be conducting an interview with a suspect. I beat back the rising rage and panic by sucking in a deep breath.

"Why did you return to Red Jacket after you got married? Why didn't you just go straight to Marquette?" Jace asked.

"That was her decision. She felt obligated to do the St. Lucy parade."

An obligation to the parade was an obligation to Arvo. Liisa wouldn't have delayed her own plans to make him happy if she'd been afraid of Arvo Maki. The realization was a calming one. I looked at Reid.

"If Liisa was planning to leave town for good, where was her suitcase?"

Both men looked at me uncomprehendingly.

"Her what?" Reid finally said.

"I didn't know Liisa, but I know girls. She wouldn't have left the Makis' house without a comb and brush, lipstick and fresh underwear. There was no suitcase at the scene. There wasn't even a purse." I kept my eyes on the younger man.

"I didn't take her stuff," he said, sounding, finally, like a belligerent teenager. "There was nothing in that sauna but her and a rock."

"The sheriff will think the same as Hatti," Jace said, heavily. "So will a jury. The evidence is closing in around you, Reid. Either you killed that girl, or someone is setting you up."

He looked frightened for a minute but quickly regained his composure.

"It's that. The second thing you said."

Jace's face appeared to be etched in stone.

"No more jokes. We've got some serious work to do."

Jace and I looked at each other. For once, we were in complete accord.

"First thing we've got to do," I said, "is find the suitcase."

Several hours later, as soon as the darkness thinned enough for us to see the path, Jace and I started down the mountain. Reid, on Jace's advice, decided to stay in the Porkies for another day or two. I thought it was a good call. As soon as Sheriff Clump got the idea of Reid Night Wind in his head, it would be all over except the crying. Clump would declare a slam dunk, Reid would be arrested and the investigation would be shut down. We needed to find the real killer, and we needed to do it soon.

I realized, with some surprise, that I'd decided Reid hadn't killed Liisa. I knew I'd have to change my tune if evidence emerged that was more than circumstantial, but I was comfortable with the presumption of innocence, and I hoped we could prove it.

Despite my physical and emotional fatigue, I thought hard as we slipped and slid down the mountain, and by the time we'd begun to thaw in the blessed warmth of the truck, I'd formulated a plan.

"I want to take a look inside Jalmer Pelonen's cabin."

"You can't. You're a duly sworn-in cop, and I'm an officer of the law. Breaking and entering is out. Besides, any evidence we found wouldn't be admitted in court. We need a search warrant."

"Don't be such a lawyer. If we apply for a search warrant, it will take too long, and, worse, we'll have Clump all over us like black flies on the side of a barn. Anyway, it isn't breaking and entering if the owner gives you a key."

My phone interrupted my diatribe. It had to be Lars. "He must have gotten in touch with Jalmer," I said, before I answered.

But it wasn't my ex-brother-in-law.

"*Hyva*," Arvo said. There was a new heaviness in his voice. "I wanted to let you know the jig is up, eh? Somehow Clump found out, and he's taking charge. The meat wagon's on its way."

"You promised me another day." I knew I sounded like a whiney three-year-old.

"I'm sorry, Hatti-girl. He found out. You know the grapevine."

I did know the grapevine. It would have made Ernest and Julio Gallo proud.

"I must go. I have to get my beautiful girl ready."

The raw grief in his voice triggered all my compassion. I felt even more certain that Arvo hadn't killed the girl he'd considered a surrogate daughter. I hung up and reported the news to Jace.

"Damn."

"I know, but the good news is that since I'm officially off the case, nothing I do is official, ergo I can break into Jalmer's cabin."

"I thought you said you had a key."

"It's good to have a backup plan."

Jace followed my directions, bypassing the Red Jacket exit on 26 and continuing north. We passed the green-and-white metal signs for Frog Creek, where the sheriff's office was located, and the hand-lettered sign for Rimrocks, one of the many ghost towns in Copper County that had started life as a thriving community of miners. I shivered.

"Turn up the heat if you're cold."

"I'm not cold. I'm sad. I hate the way towns and people just kind of disappear from the Keweenaw."

"You mean the miners? Cheer up. They'd all be dead by now, anyway."

"That makes me feel much better."

He shrugged. "Life is economics. In the case of the Keweenaw, the economy was based on natural resources, which meant at some point they were bound to run out. There was never any hope for permanent wealth and prosperity up here."

"So what are people supposed to do?"

"Move. They're supposed to follow the jobs."

I thought about the community of my youth and now, of my future. I knew Jace was right. Schools were closing, businesses folding, people moving. At some point, in the not-too-distant future, nature would reclaim the Keweenaw. At some point. Not yet.

We finally reached Ahmeek, a collection of dilapidated homes with the ubiquitous steeply pitched roof-lines and the saunas that looked like tumors attached to the side or back. The old logging road that led to Jalmer's cabin was undedicated and unplowed, and the pickup struggled in the eighteen inches of virgin snow. Finally Jace turned into the driveway that led from the spur to an open carport. The bay where Jalmer's truck should have been looked like a first grader's missing front tooth. Next to it was a pile of neatly stacked firewood and, hanging from a hook on one wall, was a snow shovel.

"Okay, Columbo," Jace said, turning off the motor. "We're here. What's next?"

I flashed him a grin, hopped out of the cab and sank into a foot-and-a-half of snow. A minute later I'd found the small door that had been carved into the side of the house and was protected by the carport.

"What the hell is that?" Jace asked, from behind me.

"Milk chute." I explained the local custom. He rolled his eyes but took the key out of my hand and made sure he was the first person through the door. After three steps he stopped so fast that I ran into him.

"Good Lord," he whispered.

"What? What?" I danced around behind him, trying to get a look at whatever he'd found, which, judging by his reaction, was probably Jalmer Pelonen lying in a pool of his own blood. Jace stepped aside so I could see the blinking lights on the sophisticated looking banks of computers.

"Geez Louise," I breathed. "It's the bridge of the Starship Enterprise."

Chapter Twelve

Since Jace has almost as much tech savvy as my niece, I left him to check out Jalmer's computers while I examined the rest of the cabin.

It didn't take long. There was a narrow galley kitchen, a couple of small bedrooms, a postage-stamp size bathroom, a washing machine and a clothesline, and, of course, a small wood-burning sauna. If it hadn't been for the computers, I'd have suspected Jalmer of being a devotee of Henry David Thoreau. I picked through the drawers and closets, finding only a few pieces of men's clothing, all of them clean and folded or hung neatly on hangers. Next to one of the twin-sized beds was a snapshot mounted in a wooden frame. It reminded me of the photo I'd seen in Pauline's bedroom except this time the girl was much younger. Tears pricked the backs of my eyes, and I carried it back to the living room.

"Find anything?"

"The refrigerator's pretty well cleaned out except for venison and rabbit in the freezer. There's no milk, which makes sense since he's gone down to Lake Gogebic."

"What's the photo?" I handed it to him. He looked at it for a long moment, apparently studying the radiant face of the blonde woman and the cherub countenance of the blonde child.

"Liisa and her mother?"

I nodded. Even as a baby her classical features had been striking. "It tells us one thing. Jalmer loves his daughter."

"Which doesn't mean he didn't kill her," Jace said.

I shook my head. "I can't believe in Jalmer Pelonen as the killer."

"Has it occurred to you," Jace said, not unkindly, "that you can't believe in anybody as the killer? And yet the girl is dead. I wonder what happened to the wealthy wife. Maybe Pelonen killed her for her money."

"Are you crazy? Look at the smile on her face. Who do you think was taking the picture?"

"There's no proof that it was Pelonen."

I didn't bother to argue. I peered at the computer.

"It's the same set-up I got earlier this year."

The comment made me sad. Life had gone on for Jace after our break-up. I forced my thoughts back to the issue.

"Why would Jalmer Pelonen need a set-up like this? And how could he afford it?"

"Good questions, and I've got no answers. I can't even get very deep into his system. Everything's password protected." He glanced at me. "Apparently the Keweenaw disregard for security doesn't extend to the cyberworld."

I thought about that. "Maybe he's a spy. Or a drug runner who got on the wrong side of somebody. Maybe his erstwhile partners killed Liisa in retribution."

"Maybe," Jace drawled, "he doesn't want anybody to see his online porn sites. Whatever. I'd like to get in."

"Maybe we can guess the password."

"Seriously?"

"Sure. People usually choose something obvious, something they won't forget. Try sauna, Suomi, fish and beer."

The keys clicked under his quick fingers. "No, no, no, no and no."

"*Pulla,* peninsula, Finland, Kalevala. Snow."

More clicking. "Negative."

"Lake, trout, woods." I broke off as inspiration struck. "Try Liisa."

"Bingo," he said. I heard the disappointment in his voice and knew he was extrapolating. He thought it was one more nail in Reid's coffin. "Never mind. I need another password to get past the menu. Wait. Look at this." I peered over his shoulder at the list of files, then read them aloud.

"Disaster Preparedness, Survival, Be Ready, Secession, Weapons, Sharpshooters, Militia."

"I'd say at minimum he's a survivalist, possibly a vigilante. It's pretty certain he has a working knowledge of guns."

"She wasn't killed with a gun."

"We don't know how she was killed."

"There aren't any guns in the cabin."

"He sounds like a conspiracy theorist. He's probably got his guns hidden in the floorboards." He looked thoughtful. "If he's a member of a militia, he's probably made some well-armed enemies."

"You think the attack on Liisa came from outside the community?"

He flashed me a quick grin. "Don't get your hopes up. Whoever killed her had to know the house, the Makis' schedule and about Liisa's intended rendezvous in the sauna. And my money is on someone who knew about Reid and figured out just exactly how to set him up."

"You think it was Arvo."

"I'm sorry, Hatti."

"And yet, Arvo would have no financial reason for killing Liisa."

"We don't know that."

"But we can find out. I'll just get ahold of Jussi & Jussi."

"What," he asked, shutting down the computer and getting to his feet, "the hell is that?"

"A law firm. Everybody in Red Jacket uses them when they need a lawyer. With two million dollars at stake you can bet your boots they have something to do with the Pelonen family." I watched as he grabbed a kitchen towel and quickly and thoroughly wiped down everything we'd touched.

"You'd have made an award-winning burglar," I said, after he'd returned the wiped-down key to the milk chute.

"It's always nice to be appreciated."

Despite the light exchange we didn't talk much on the way back to town. I couldn't shake off the sadness I felt for Jalmer, who was facing the most terrible news possible for a parent. I couldn't shake off the worry for Arvo, either, or for Reid. And I was worried about myself. I was enjoying spending time with Jace way too much.

"Hatti," he said, as he pulled up in front of Bait & Stitch. My heart fluttered. Was he going to say something profound? Something along the lines of how much he'd missed me and how good it was to spend time with me again? "I need Sonya Stillwater's address."

The jealousy that surged through me left me feeling weak, nauseated and disgusted with myself. Sonya was beautiful, elegant, kind and exactly the kind of woman Jace should have married in the first place. "Why?"

"I want to talk to her about her examination of the body. I'm not going to ask her out on a date."

I shrugged. "Do whatever you want." I gave him her address on Third Street. "She lives above the office."

He looked amused, and I knew he was once again reading my mind.

"Convenient for a quickie, huh?"

I couldn't even laugh at myself. I slid out of the high truck cab and slammed the door. A moment later I jerked open the shop's front door hoping there were no customers and came face to face with a pair of crystal blue eyes that had lost their twinkle.

"What's wrong Hatti-girl?" Arvo asked.

"Conniption fit," Einar muttered from his stool in the corner. "She needs husband."

My cheeks flamed. It was bad enough being in a jealous temper. It was hateful to get caught. I shook my head.

"I'm fine. Just tired."

Arvo looked at me sideways. "Where have you been, Hatti-girl?"

I opened and shut my mouth like a codfish as I remembered, belatedly, that I was bound to secrecy about Reid Night Wind.

"Nowhere special. Just doing a little poking around."

Arvo shook his head. "Leave it to Clump," he said, heavily. "It's not your problem anymore."

I'd temporarily forgotten that, too.

"Were you looking for me?"

"Hmm? Oh, yes, yes." Arvo frowned as he felt the pockets of his overcoat until he came up with a folded piece of paper. It was such a familiar gesture that I had to smile. Pauline was always making lists for him, then tucking them into his pockets. He was the big concept guy, and she was the detail person. It was, I thought, the secret of their success.

"Doc Laitimaki is doing the autopsy," he said, before consulting the list. "I thought you'd like to know." Viktor Laitimaki, a general practitioner, was one of five physicians who shared autopsy responsibilities for the three counties on the Keweenaw. He'd been our family doctor since I was born. I was glad it was Doc's rotation. He'd come up with some answers. He'd also come up with the news about the pregnancy, and there would be no way to protect Arvo from finding out about it. Should I tell him now? I really couldn't. Not after I'd promised Pauline.

The investigation, I thought, involved too many secrets.

"Your mama and papa be home *Keskiviikko*," Einar chimed in. "Dey call dis afternoon."

"Wednesday," Arvo repeated, his eyes glittering with unshed tears, "in time for the funeral. I am going to lay our girl to rest in the Excelsior—white with carved rosebuds. Top of the line."

He'd already told me, but I didn't point it out. I just patted his heavy shoulder. After a moment he read from Pauline's note.

"Something about a necklace," he muttered. "I am supposed to ask you about an Indian necklace."

For a minute, I couldn't catch my breath.

"Liisa had an Indian necklace," he said, assuming, because of my silence, that I didn't understand. "Clump asked Pauly for it, but she didn't know where it was. She thought you might have found it in Liisa's room."

"Clump asked Pauline? But who told him about the necklace?"

Arvo looked at the note. "It doesn't say." He screwed up his face in an effort of memory. "I don't remember it, either, but it might be a present from the Night Wind boy."

I'd forgotten until that moment that Arvo had been present the night Reid and Liisa had met. Our efforts to keep his name out of the investigation had been doomed to fail from the get-go.

"Reid. I believe he was the baby's papa."

I gaped at him. Arvo knew about the baby?

"Liisa was going to have a baby," he explained. His face collapsed in grief. "It would have been our grandbaby. Pauly's and mine."

"But Pauline didn't know about the baby. She found out after Sonya examined the body. She made us promise not to tell you."

"*Joo*. My Liisa, she told me on Thanksgiving because I found the pregnancy test box, eh. She thought I would be mad, but I wasn't. I didn't care that she wasn't married. I wanted to take care of her and the little one, too. They could have stayed with us. They would have been our family."

"But why would Pauline tell me she didn't know?"

"Liisa was saving the news to tell Pauly on her birthday."

"But Pauline's birthday is in the summer."

"No, no. On Liisa's birthday. Her eighteenth. We shouldn't have waited. Now Pauly will never have the happiness, just the sorrow." He started to walk toward the door, and I went with him.

"Arvo," I said, "did Liisa ever talk about leaving Red Jacket?"

"*Joo.* Next year. She wanted to go to Marquette to study music."

"But she planned to stay with you until then?" He nodded.

"Did it ever seem to you she was afraid of something?"

"Spiders. Dogs. She was a bit timid. Like you with worms."

Spiders and dogs. Hardly enough motivation for a runaway elopement. None of this made sense. I had to keep pressing, but I needed to choose my words carefully. I wondered if he knew about Liisa's inheritance and knew I couldn't mention it. Not yet.

"Someone," I said, carefully, "suggested Liisa was planning to leave town that night. The thirteenth."

"No, that is not right, Henrikki. She was going to sing St. Lucy the next day."

The distress on his face hurt my heart. He looked so old and tired that I simply couldn't ask him any more questions. Not now. I opened the door, which let a gust of cold, snowy air into the room.

"Arvo," I said, "is there anything I can do for you?"

His eyebrows lifted as if I'd reminded him of something.

"Pauline needs three dozen yellow roses for the grave blanket.

Can you ask Sofi?"

I nodded. "I'll bring them up to the house myself."

After Arvo left I took a quick look at the mail and asked Einar if there were any messages for me.

"*Joo.* Miss Irene wants yarn."

"Did she say which yarn?"

He nodded. "*Joo.*"

"Did you write it down?"

He shook his head.

"Okay. Good job. Did she say anything else?"

He closed his eyes, then recited from his excellent memory. " 'God hath clothed me with the garments of salvation; he hath covered me with the robe of righteousness, Isaiah, 61:10.' "

My laughter included a tinge of exasperation. How was it that Einar could remember a Bible verse word for word but he couldn't write down Adrialfil Knitcol or Berroco Fuji in pine needle?

"Any other messages?"

"Sofi husband called."

Lars! He must have gotten in touch with Jalmer Pelonen. I wondered why he hadn't called on my cell, but the mystery was solved when I checked it. The battery had died. I'd call Lars just as soon as I delivered Arvo's message to my sister.

Sofi's shop smelled of freshly cut flowers and an odd combination of peppermint and eggnog, the two flavors she mixed with chocolate to create her holiday fudge.

I greeted Charlie at the cash register and waved to the shoppers, then I slipped behind the counter to cut myself a square of peanut butter-chocolate. It was always good for a mood boost, and I figured I deserved it. Sleuthing was hard work. Sleuthing with an ex, even an almost-ex, was beyond stressful. I licked my fingers and ducked into the backroom.

Sofi's shop is a narrow rectangle like mine, but where most of

mine is showroom, most of hers is backroom. Her three spacious coolers are nearly always filled with buckets of freshly cut
flowers, and her shelves are neatly stacked with containers,
spools of wire and ribbon, Styrofoam inserts, and all the rest of
the paraphernalia needed for flower arranging.

She was working on an arrangement in a ceramic bowl that
used snapdragons, carnations and delicate yellow rosebuds.
She'd fastened her wheat colored hair with a scrunchy, and it
spewed forth from the top of her head like a fountain. Her face
was rosy and moist from exertion.

"Everybody and their Aunt Sadie has been in here today
either ordering centerpieces for Christmas or flowers for Liisa
Pelonen's funeral."

"You mean everybody knows?"

Sofi nodded, a gesture that made her hair fountain dance.
"They know she's dead. They don't know she may have been
murdered. Listen, could you strip the leaves off those asters?
And maybe the daisies, too?"

As I had no eye for floral arranging, my only value to her was
driving the delivery truck or, in a pinch like this, stripping. I got
to work.

"How was your sleepover?"

I lifted my eyebrows. "You make it sound like a slumber party.
It wasn't. It was a fact-finding mission."

"A fact-finding sleepover. With your ex-husband."

I didn't bother to argue or to correct her accuracy. I knew
she just didn't want me to get hurt again. I told her about Reid
Night Wind's marriage to Liisa and about the trust fund.

"Looks like he's our guy."

"Jace thinks Reid's been set up."

Sofi's big blue eyes held mine. "What do you think?"

I shrugged. "According to what we know it seems almost
impossible that the killer could be anybody else, but that makes

me suspicious. The whole thing's just a little too neat."

My sister sighed. "You're thinking about fiction, Hatti. This is real life where the person who is most likely to be the killer is the killer. Is he the baby's father?"

"He says not."

"Does he have any explanation for the St. Lucy costume?"

"No. None."

"He married her for money, honey. What does that say about him?"

I refused to put it into words. I was pretty sure Reid was ashamed of the impulse to take money from the girl, and I thought that, in the end, he wouldn't. I believed he'd been fond of her, and I didn't think he'd done it primarily for the money. He'd seen a girl who was frightened and alone, and he'd stepped in to help. In a way.

"You're romanticizing him, Hatti. I know you. He's your ex-brother-in-law, and you're trying to protect him."

"I don't think so. I think I'm willing to accept the truth. I just don't want to be manipulated into accepting what isn't the truth."

Sofi worked with the flowers for a minute, then spoke again. "Will he inherit the whole trust fund now?"

"I surely to goodness hope not."

"Are you going to tell Sheriff Clump about Reid?"

I wouldn't have. It didn't matter now. "Somebody already told him. Arvo asked me about the dream-catcher necklace. He said the sheriff asked Pauline about it. It's only a quick hop and a jump from the dream catcher to Reid."

Sofi's hands went still, and she looked at me.

"I think you should find out who tipped off the sheriff."

I nodded. "It's a question worth asking."

"There's some other interesting news," Sofi said. "Diane was in this morning to place an order for wedding flowers. It seems

Barb and Matti Murso are getting married after all, and they've moved the ceremony from June to March so they can honeymoon during spring break at the Ellsworth Cheese Curd Festival over in Wisconsin."

I raised my eyebrows. "Last week Matti was in love with someone else."

"Yeah, well, I don't think this is about love as much as it's about grabbing an opportunity before it slips away again."

I stripped the last of the flowers and wiped my hands on my jeans.

"If that's enough daisies, I think I'll go over to the Gas 'n Go and have a little talk with Matti. Oh, and Pauline wants three dozen roses for the grave blanket. I said I'd deliver 'em."

"I can do it."

I shook my head thinking about the missing suitcase. "Just call me when they're ready. I'd like a chance to take another look at Liisa's room."

CHAPTER THIRTEEN

The Gas 'n Go, a convenience store-slash-service station owned and operated by Tauno Murso, sold motor oil, coffee that tasted like motor oil, red vines, gum, canned soup, boxed cereal and milk that was always perilously close to its expiration date.

I found Tauno where he seemed to spend most of his time, under the chassis of a pickup.

"Mr. Murso?"

"Mita?"

He responded with the Finnish word for "what," which was encouraging, but he did not come out from under the vehicle, and I found it a little awkward to introduce myself to his left boot. I did it anyway.

"I'm Hatti Lehtinen, and I'd like to speak with Matti."

There was a long pause while he digested my words. Did he know why I was there? Was he afraid his son was in trouble with the law? Or was he working on a mechanical problem that took up all the space in his cerebrum? The response came at long last.

"Ei tanne." Not here.

I tried again. "Where can I find him?"

"Mita?"

I sighed. This was going nowhere fast. I doubted whether Tauno would be this uncooperative with Pops. But, of course, they were both part of the Finnish good ole boys club.

"Don't bother Tauno, Umlaut. Can't you see he's busy?"

I jumped, not just because I hadn't heard him come in behind me but because he'd used Jace's nickname for me. Had he known? Of course he hadn't known. I stifled a self-deprecatory laugh. It was a fine nickname, but it wasn't all that original. I produced a smile for Max.

"What're you doing here?"

"I saw you come in, figured you wanted to talk to Matti and deduced that you'd need a little help with translation."

I knew he wasn't talking about Finnish to English but about the great communication gap that exists between taciturn Finnish males like Tauno and other folks.

"As it happens," he continued, "I believe I can help you. Please, climb into my carriage, er, truck."

"Why?"

"I know where to find Matti."

I got into the front seat. His pickup was much nicer than the one Jace had borrowed from his grandfather. This one was a late model that was spacious, comfortable and warm. As always with Max, I relaxed. There was something solid about him. He always seemed to know what he was doing, and I didn't worry about what he was doing when I wasn't with him.

"Whither bound?"

He laughed and put the truck in gear. "Hockey practice."

Of course. The Copper County High Muskrats hockey team is by far the most popular spectator sport in Red Jacket, probably because it's the only one. Like many small schools in the U.P., we had to give up our football team years ago, but hockey was the life's blood of Northern Michigan, and it would be the last thing to go.

"What's your connection to the team?"

"I keep score at the games."

"You play hockey? I thought you were from Texas?"

"We've got ice. Indoors."

I laughed, then relaxed into the leather seat as Max easily navigated the blocks to the park. I felt safe for the first time since Jace Night Wind had turned up at my door, so safe that I must have gone to sleep, because I felt a feather light touch on my cheek and heard Max saying, "Hey, sleepyhead."

I sat up. "I'm so sorry, Max."

"Rough night?"

"Long night," I said. Then I blushed, remembering our interrupted "date" of the night before.

"I want to apologize about Saturday night, too."

"There's no need. That guy really your husband?"

"For the moment."

"Oh, like that, is it? I don't think he got the memo."

"He got it all right. He wrote it."

There was a serious expression in Max's warm brown eyes. "I think he may want to issue a new directive."

"He's not here because of me. He's worried about his brother."

"You mean Liisa Pelonen's boyfriend?"

I jumped. "How do you know that?"

"Everybody knows that. It was on Betty Ann's show this morning. No, I'm kidding about that, but it's all over town. He's everybody's favorite candidate for number one murder suspect." He paused. "That what you wanted to talk to me about the other night?"

I was ashamed of myself now. I'd taken on the responsibility of investigating Liisa's death, and I'd immediately handed it off to everyone in sight.

"I wanted to ask you some questions. Sonya Stillwater said you used to be some kind of investigator." He looked out the window at the rink, where the hockey players were finishing their scrimmage.

"Federal marshal."

146

"I intended to pick your brain. Silly, wasn't it?"

"Not at all," he said, turning back to me. "My brain is at your disposal. You investigating in your capacity as police chief?"

"Not anymore. Sheriff Clump found out and took over. I am still trying to make sense of it just for my own satisfaction."

"Trying to save your brother-in-law?"

I shrugged, a little uncomfortable with that description. "I'd like to make sure justice is done."

"Meaning you think he's been framed?"

"I think it's a possibility."

"That why you want to talk to Matti? Because he had a thing for Liisa?"

I nodded.

"I thought he might be able to tell me something about the girl."

He nodded in the direction of a tall, gangly figure who was headed toward the truck. Matti Murso was carrying his helmet under one arm and his stick in the other. Other assorted gear stuck out of the large canvas bag he wore across his back. He had blond hair, dreamy blue eyes and a few pimples, and he looked a generation younger than Reid Night Wind. "There's your man."

"Hey, Max," Matti called out, in a friendly voice. "You comin' to the game this weekend? We're gonna clobber Menominee."

The smile on Matti's face disappeared like the sun under a passing cumulus cloud, and I realized he knew why I was here. For a minute I thought he'd refuse to talk to me, but he got into the truck, no doubt out of respect for Max.

"I want to ask you a few questions about Liisa Pelonen," I said, gently. "I imagine you've heard that she's dead."

He nodded. His face looked closed and sad. And, suddenly, older.

"Barb said it was an accident."

147

"It may have been an accident," I agreed, "we don't know yet. Since I'm taking my dad's place as police chief, I have to find out everything I can about her and her friends and what she did that day."

"It was her birthday."

"I know."

"There's no sense talking to me. I didn't even see her."

"You didn't go to the parade?"

"No."

"Or the Snowflake Dance?"

He stared at me. "No. She wasn't going to be there. I heard she was sick."

He might not have gone to the parade, but he knew exactly what Liisa had been doing all day up until she complained of a sore throat. And this was the boy who was supposed to marry someone else in March.

"Can you think of anyone who would want to kill Liisa?"

He shook his head and stared down at his hands.

"Can you think of anyone who was mad at her? Did she have any enemies?"

"I don't know if she had enemies. I don't know if she had friends, either. She didn't talk a lot. Not to anybody."

"Did she talk at the Homecoming Dance?"

"She was bored. She only went to please Mrs. Maki."

"What about after the dance?" He shot me a quick, agonized glance, and I knew the question unsettled him, but I had to try to find out whether he'd been the baby's father.

"What about it?"

"Did you take her directly home, or did you go out to Nama-gok?" Max's fishing camp, possibly unknown to him, doubled as the local make-out spot.

"We drove over there but didn't stay. She said the Makis wanted her home by midnight."

I couldn't think of a way to ask him if they'd had sex.

"Did Liisa ever tell you she was afraid of someone in Red Jacket?"

"No."

"Did she seem afraid?"

"No. Just bored."

I sighed. I was going to have to do it. "Matti, did you know Liisa was expecting a baby?"

His face turned the color of cream cheese. "I'm not the father."

"I didn't say you were."

"Well, I'm not. I'd have married her though. She didn't want me."

His words cut me to the heart.

"You know you don't have to marry anyone. Not yet. You're still very young."

"Barb wants to get married now."

"Do you?"

He lifted his hands, palms out in a helpless gesture that clearly meant it didn't matter one way or the other.

"You loved Liisa, didn't you? Do you think Barb will be happy married to a man who loves someone else?"

"She's not thinking of that. She just wants to get married."

My heart ached for him. "All right. Is there anything else you can tell me?"

"Just that I wasn't surprised when I heard she was dead."

"Why not?"

"She liked to get people stirred up. She liked danger."

It sounded as if Matti and Reid had known different girls. Who, I wondered, was the real Liisa Pelonen? And who had she gotten "stirred up" enough to kill her?

Dusk had darkened the sky when Max pulled up in front of my parents' home. I could see the lights inside, and I knew Sofi and Elli and Charlie would be there waiting for me. Even though I was beyond tired and more than a little discouraged, I felt a comforting sense of belonging. My friends and family had helped me through the worst time in my life, and now they were helping me again—both with my personal struggle and the murder investigation. I looked forward to laying out the pieces in front of them to see what they thought. I glanced at the man next to me and felt a similar surge of affection. He was part of my new world, and suddenly I wanted him to become part of my tribe.

"Have you got dinner plans?"

He looked surprised. "What do you have in mind?"

I nodded at the house. "Elli and Sofi are setting up a little smorgasbord of leftovers from the festival, and we'd love to have you join us. I should warn you the conversation will almost certainly center on the investigation."

"My kind of conversation." He hesitated though, and I thought I understood.

"Jace won't be there. Here, I mean." I didn't add that he'd gone off in search of Sonya Stillwater and was doubtless still with her. And then I realized it was Sonya he was concerned about. "No one else will be there either."

Max nodded. "I'd like to contribute something to the party."

"I'm sure there's enough food for all of Copper County. All we're lacking is a Christmas tree."

The brown eyes sparkled. "Christmas trees, I've got. Want me to just bring one over, or do you want the thrill of slogging through the knee-deep snow to pick it out yourself?"

I needed a memory to wipe out the ones from the shrapnel-fest that had been last Christmas.

"I want to pick it out. Do you mind if we bring someone along?"

Twenty minutes later Charlie, Larry and I piled back into

Max's truck, and when we returned, red-cheeked and starving, we were the possessors of a ten-foot white pine. Elli had invited the usual suspects: Aunt Ianthe, Miss Irene, the Sorensens, Einar, Arvo and Pauline, so the investigation was off the table, and everyone agreed to help decorate the tree. All in all, I was glad. I could use a break from murder, and, besides, it was a good chance to clean up before Mom and Pops arrived.

After a supper of leftovers embellished with Elli's special omelets made of eggs, butter, onions, potatoes, Gruyere cheese and *Joululimppu,* we gathered around the tree in the parlor and dug out the Christmas decorations Mom had packed up so carefully the year before. Sofi set the crèche up on the mantelpiece, Elli and the aunts hunted for the straw reindeer, the wooden gnomes, and the hand-knit red and white Christmas balls that portrayed all the symbols, including St. Lucy. Einar and the Reverend Sorensen hung the lights, and Max lifted Charlie up high enough to place a tin star on the topmost branch.

When the tree was decorated, I produced the pièce de résistance traditionally applied by my mother. I flocked the tree with a spray can of artificial snow while we sang Christmas carols in the key of C, accompanied by Aunt Ianthe. We were just finishing that old favorite, *Sylvian Joululaulu,* or Sylvia's Christmas Song, when Arvo's cellphone rang. As we heard the first tinny notes of the polka, we all quieted down. No one had really forgotten what was going on in our community. Arvo stayed in the parlor, but his responses were monosyllabic. I waited impatiently for news.

"That was Doc," he said. Harsh lines bracketed his mouth, like human parentheses. "Liisa was not killed with a blow to the head. He believes she fainted, and her heart stopped."

I digested that for a moment.

"But, dear," Pauline said, her long face drawn with sorrow,

"people faint all the time. They don't die from it."

Arvo slipped his arm around her, absently.

"Doc said it was something called 'syncope.'" Arvo pronounced it "sin-co-pee." "The faint can be caused by a fever, by panic, by anything, but in some people the heartbeat slows for too long, and it finally stops." He paused. "Resulting in death. Doc asked if she'd had any history of heart problems."

No one knew. Of course not. Liisa had come to Red Jacket without any family. She'd been, essentially, an outsider.

Miss Irene spoke softly, reverently.

" 'O death, where is thy sting? O grave, where is thy victory? First Corinthians 15:55.'"

I knew she meant to be comforting. Death, to a devoted Christian, was not the end. It seemed like the end for Liisa, though. Anger slammed into me, and fury pounded in my veins. Someone had robbed that girl of, perhaps, dozens of Christmas celebrations like the one we were having. She wouldn't be a singer or a mother or a wife or anything. And that someone was about to get off the hook because Doc couldn't figure out how she was killed.

Not on my watch, I thought, as I watched Arvo and Pauline clinging to one another for a comfort that clearly eluded them. I intended to identify Liisa's murderer even if it turned out to be Reid Night Wind.

Everyone was still trying to interpret the news when the doorbell rang. Max, standing by the tree and thus closest to the door, answered it. I was close behind him, and I saw his muscular body tense as he admitted the two on the doorstep.

Sonya Stillwater stepped into the room first. Her color was brilliant from the cold, and her midnight blue eyes shone. The long, blue-black hair shone in the glow of the foyer lamp, and her lovely smile seemed to light up the room. I saw the long-fingered male hand of her companion, as he easily, naturally, removed her long, wool coat. My gaze traveled up to his face, and the slate gray eyes focused steadily on me. Mrs. Sorensen spoke in a low voice, but I could hear her plainly.

"Don't they make an enchanting couple?"

"Forgive me for being so late," Sonya said, after a minute. "We just attended a birth."

" 'For Unto Us a Child is Born,' " Miss Irene said, joyfully. "Isaiah:7."

Sonya smiled at Miss Irene. "It was almost as much of a miracle as the one in the manger. Jace was a knight in shining armor." She flashed a brilliant smile at him.

"Rusted armor," he murmured, modestly. His eyes were still on me. Was he sending me a message? I couldn't think straight for the jealousy roiling in my stomach.

Sonya, who was usually quiet in a large crowd, shook her head.

"Jace was in my office when I got a panicked call from Cindy Gray Squirrel on the rez. She's young and was very scared. She's had some complications, and I wanted her to deliver in the hospital, but she had no way to get there. Jace drove us. And then he stayed with Cindy for the entire birth." She flashed another smile at him. This time he grinned back at her.

Elli, in her quiet, efficient way, drew the newcomers into the room and got them served with plates of food and mugs of coffee even as they answered a series of eager questions.

"She wanted a stranger to stay during childbirth?" Mrs. Sorensen asked.

"Cindy trusted Jace because he is Chief Joseph's grandson," Sonya explained. "She asked him to give the baby an Ojibwe blessing."

Jace grimaced, comically. "I didn't know one. Sonya fed me the lines."

I could just see the partnership in the intimacy of a hospital delivery room with the aura of new life—new beginnings—all around them. I struggled to remember that Sonya was one of my closest friends, that I loved her. The plain fact was that I was jealous, a feeling that was at least as painful as rejection. The small part of my mind that wasn't eaten up with the emotion recognized that the green-eyed monster was powerful enough to incite murder. Not that I would have killed Sonya. I'd have sent her on a world cruise, though. I'd have sent her away.

Aunt Ianthe asked for more details, Miss Irene blessed the story with more Bible references and everyone else praised Jace for his heroic effort with Cindy Gray Wolf whom, I told myself spitefully, none of them even knew. My own feelings horrified and disgusted me, and I was glad to hear the doorbell ring again. Any diversion was welcome. This time Charlie answered it, and I heard her joyful shout.

"Daddy!"

My niece wrapped her beanpole frame around Lars. She looked like a tightly wound tetherball, and my eyes flew to Sofi's face. It had turned to stone.

CHAPTER FOURTEEN

"Hello, Snork Maiden. Been up to mischief?"

" 'His mischief shall return upon his own head, and his violent dealing shall come down upon his own pate. Psalms 7:16.' "

"An apt choice, dear," Aunt Ianthe told her friend. After a respectful pause, Charlie started to chatter.

"Max took Hatti and Larry and I to get the Christmas tree."

"Me," Lars corrected. "Max took Hatti and me."

"And Larry," Charlie told him, with an impish grin. He grinned back and set her on her feet. "Come into the kitchen with me," she said, pulling on his hand. "You look like you're starving."

Lars cast a quick glance at Sofi, but she had turned to say something to Sonya, so he looked at me. I thought I read a summons in his emerald eyes, so I followed father and daughter out to the kitchen. Had he talked to Jalmer Pelonen? My heart raced, and my jealousy was (almost) forgotten.

"I'm really not hungry," Lars told Charlie, gently. "I do need to talk to Hatti."

"Is it about Liisa's murder?" Charlie-the-little-girl morphed into Charlie the intelligent young woman. "I'm in on the investigation, you know, Dad."

I nodded. "She's given me some valuable information about Liisa's experiences with the school crowd. I think she can handle a report on your conversation with Jalmer."

A faint frown developed between Lars's black brows. He studied his daughter's face and apparently made a decision.

"All right, but this is confidential information, Snork. Don't tell anyone until Aunt Hatti gives you the go-ahead." She nodded solemnly, then held out her little finger. "Pinky swear." When the ritual was finished, Lars turned back to me.

"I didn't have a conversation with Jalmer," he said. "I found him. Toes up in the Ontonagon County morgue. He's been there more than a week."

My stomach somersaulted, and I glanced at Charlie, who said, "Holy wha!" a phrase she'd learned from Pops.

"How did it happen?"

"Car accident. At least, that's what the police report says."

I stared at him in dismay. "You don't believe it?"

"His truck went off the cliff road and incinerated. There's no evidence to show otherwise, but I was curious that he'd had no I.D. on him. It made me wonder. So I hiked down to the wreck to check it out. I found a blown-off fender with a piece of wood wired to it. I think it was the remains of a sticky bomb."

"You think he was murdered," I squeaked.

"What's a sticky bomb?" Charlie asked.

Lars had no chance to answer. The door from the butler's pantry opened, and we were joined by Pauline, Arvo and Jace.

"I'm afraid we have to leave," Pauline said to me. "Thank you for having us tonight, Hatti."

"Wait," her husband said, looking from me to Lars and back again. "Something's happened, hasn't it?"

I was reluctant to share the information until I'd had a chance to digest it, but I could think of no reason to hold back from either the Makis or Jace. I nodded at Lars, who told them about finding Jalmer's body in the morgue.

"Lars found the remains of a sticky bomb on a fender from Jalmer's truck," I added.

"He was murdered?" Pauline's voice trembled, and she looked about to collapse. Arvo put his arm around her, but his attention was focused on Lars.

"What's a sticky bomb?" he asked, unconsciously echoing Charlie's question.

"A homemade explosive used by terrorists targeting a single vehicle." The words came from Jace. "You can get the ingredients—bits of glass and metal, compound, and accelerant—at any hardware store, and instructions are available on the Internet. The bombs are usually detonated with a cell phone."

"A robot bomb," Charlie said.

"Geez Louise," I whispered, appalled that someone I knew would assemble and detonate a bomb meant to kill a harmless person like Jalmer Pelonen. And there was no doubt in my mind that it was someone I knew. Jalmer's death had to be linked to Liisa's death. I thought about the two-million-dollar trust fund. Had there been a financial motive, after all?

"What does it mean?" Pauline asked.

Arvo's eyes seemed to have sunk into his tired face.

"Two deaths in one week, father and daughter. It means our Liisa did not die of sincope. If Jalmer was murdered, and he was, then Liisa was murdered, too."

I heard an odd, hoarse, cracked sound and realized that Pauline was weeping, her face in her husband's shoulder. I felt an overwhelming sadness for both the Makis and pure terror for Jace. Things were looking very bad for Reid Night Wind.

The Makis left, and the rest of us returned to the parlor. What I really wanted to do was talk to Jace, to get his take on the new development, but he shrugged into his leather jacket, said goodbye to my sister and cousin, and ushered Sonya out the front door.

I wondered, sourly, if they were on their way to deliver more babies.

"Listen, Squirt," I heard Lars say, "I think you should turn this over to the sheriff. Whoever killed these two is smart and ruthless and probably crazy."

"Not crazy. I think there's a plan." I told him about the two million dollars Liisa had been eligible to collect on her birthday, Friday. I told him about the marriage, too.

His hard face softened as he listened to me and, quick as he is, grasped the implications.

"Looks like it's Reid Night Wind, honey. I'm sorry."

"I talked to him," I whispered. "I don't think he did it. I think . . . well, I think someone's trying to frame him."

"And doing a helluva job of it." His eyes narrowed. "You realize it has to be someone who knew Liisa and her father and who also knew the local routines and schedules. This is close to home, Hatti, and that makes it even more dangerous for you. You'll find yourself hard-pressed to suspect anyone you know and/or care about. I think you need to give it up."

"I can't. Sheriff Clump will pin it on Reid Night Wind."

Lars shrugged. "Maybe he did it."

"But maybe he didn't. He won't get a fair hearing. It'll be a star chamber, a kangaroo court."

He accepted my decision. It was one of the things I'd always loved about Lars. He'd always supported me, just as he supported Charlie, but he'd never tried to shield me from the consequences of my own decisions. It was the right way to parent, I thought, and I'd try to emulate it when it was my turn. I flashed on the picture of the newly formed obstetric team as they'd left together a few minutes earlier. I felt my jaw tighten and my teeth grind together. I was only jealous because it was happening in front of my face. Jace could date whomever he wanted, except for one of my best friends, and I planned to tell him so. There are boundaries in every good divorce.

"Look, I'm going to walk Charlie home, and I'm hoping to get a chance to talk to Sofi about this Christmas thing. I'll be back, shortly though. Just leave a blanket and pillow for me on the parlor sofa."

"You really think it's necessary to spend the night here?"

His emerald-colored eyes were shadowed. "Has it occurred to you that Pops's accident might have been a murder attempt?"

It hadn't. I shook my head.

"You need protection, Hatti, and I'm going to make sure you get it."

I thought about Lars's words after I let Larry out, then climbed wearily up the back stairs. He might be right, but I thought there was more to it. Was it possible that Pops's accident wasn't a failed murder attempt but a successful attempt to get the police chief out of the way? Was the goal to leave Red Jacket without any law enforcement so that when the Pelonens began to fall like bowling pins, there would be no one to investigate? Or did the perpetrator know our community well enough to figure out that we'd replace Pops with an inexperienced, figurehead law officer? I shivered. No one could have known Arvo would appoint a complete novice like me. But that wasn't true: One person would have known. I shivered again. The picture I was piecing together scared me right down to the bone. It was becoming more and more evident that the murderer was nearby, both emotionally and physically. My mind shied away from the obvious answer. It had to be wrong. Arvo had no reason for wishing Jalmer dead, and he'd loved Liisa. The motive had to be money, which led me back to Reid Night Wind, my soon-to-be-ex brother-in-law.

It had to be one or the other of them. I crawled into bed and pulled the covers over my head.

★ ★ ★ ★ ★

I must have been more exhausted than I'd realized. I didn't hear Lars return, and I got up too late to see him leave, but he'd left his footprint in the form of the perfectly folded Hudson Bay army blanket on the sofa and the note in Larry's dish that read: I-8.

As I made coffee, munched on a chunk of Trenary toast and stared out the kitchen window at the snowflakes dancing and swirling in the early morning flurries, I tried not to think too hard but to let the information I'd gathered dance and swirl, too. There seemed to me to be a couple of leads to pursue. First of all, we had to find out what had really killed Liisa. And then there was the trust fund business. And I still had no answer to the question of paternity. My mind stuck on the word.

Fatherhood. It seemed to be all over this case. Liisa had lived with her surrogate father when she was killed. Liisa's real father was killed. My stepfather had been injured. Why did Jace insist upon calling Pops my "stepfather"? The last question didn't apply to the murders, of course, any more than the question after that: Where had Jace spent the night?

I'd forgotten I'd asked Elli to introduce me to Mr. Jussi until she called to say she'd set up a lunch date for us in Hancock. I hoped he could shed a little light on the Pelonens' finances. In the meantime, I needed to focus on the other local issue: Tomorrow, Mom and Pops would return home.

I wouldn't have to worry about food. Starting this afternoon, folks would start letting themselves in with our spare key. They'd bring plastic and Pyrex containers of mouthwatering casseroles, meatloaves, salads, vegetables, bread and Christmas cookies, which they'd stack in the refrigerator or on the counter. None of the containers would be marked. There was no need. My mother knew exactly which ones belonged where. The exchange of food had been honed to a fine art in Red Jacket.

Cleaning, though, was another issue altogether, and my mother, the Upper Peninsula's answer to Heloise, would expect everything to be dusted and vacuumed, with clean sheets and towels and scrubbed floors. I groaned. Just thinking about all that cleaning made my head ache, so I poured myself another cup of coffee, wandered into the study and stared out the window. More snowflakes. I sighed, plopped down into Pops's easy chair and stared at the books lined up on the shelves. My eye was caught by the titles by Margery Allingham, Patricia Wentworth, Ngaio Marsh, P. D. James and, of course, Agatha Christie. I'd read them all at one time. I wished, fancifully, for the wisdom of those fictional detectives and their clever authors like Dorothy L. Sayers and her Lord Peter Wimsey. I picked up one of the books, titled *Strong Poison,* and suddenly I felt that ripple up my spine that sometimes heralds a panic attack. This time it was inspiration.

Poison. Was that how Liisa was killed? Had someone poisoned her? It seemed like the only answer, and yet, if she'd been poisoned, wouldn't Doc Laitimaiki have discovered that?

I opened the book and read the first page, and I didn't look up until Elli appeared in front of me. She was wearing a fashion-able gray pantsuit, a dashing red scarf and makeup.

"What are you doing?"

"I think I've figured it out. Liisa was poisoned."

"I meant, what are you doing in your pajamas?"

I glanced down at the oversized T-shirt that displayed an outline of the Upper Peninsula and the words "Will U.P. Mine?"

"We're supposed to meet Jaako Jussi in forty-five minutes, Hatti."

H-E-double hockey sticks. I exploded out of my chair and headed for the stairs, leaving Elli to let Larry out.

I thrust my legs into a pair of green corduroy jeans and my arms into a butter-yellow sweater. Not very seasonal, but a step up from a sweatshirt. A comb through the haystack on my head, a swipe of lip gloss and I was ready to join Elli in the ancient SUV she'd insisted she needed for the B&B and that Lars called the Queen Mary.

"This may not be the time to mention it," she said, shifting as we turned off Tamarack onto M-26 south, "but you forgot to deliver the yellow roses to Pauline."

I winced and promised myself I'd make it up to Sofi. Just as soon as I solved this murder.

CHAPTER FIFTEEN

"So you think Liisa was poisoned?"

Elli was able to shift and navigate through a driving snow-storm and carry on an in-depth conversation at the same time. I'd always envied her this ability.

"I do. It's the only thing that makes sense."

"But wouldn't any poison have shown up in the autopsy?"

I sighed. "That's the snag."

Elli frowned at the snow pelting the windshield.

"I'm almost sure there are arcane poisons," I said, trying to bolster my theory. "Stuff that doesn't show up on a routine autopsy. I think I remember examples of that on some of those old *Murder, She Wrote* reruns."

"That's fiction."

"The characters are fictitious, but I'm sure the murders are all plausible."

"What makes you think so?"

"Someone would complain."

"Like who, a murderer?"

"I'm going to talk to Doc as soon as I get a chance."

"Even if he says it's possible, we won't know who's behind it," Elli pointed out.

"I don't think there are that many possibilities." I told her the prevailing theory about Pops's accident.

"That means it's someone in the inner circle."

"Yep."

"Hatti," she said, after a few miles, "do you think it's Arvo?"

"No." My response was too quick. She glanced at me.

"I think," she said, "that the murderer is someone we know, someone who knows us. It was good that you had a bodyguard last night. You should have one every night." She paused. "So where did he sleep?"

The odd question matched the odd tone in her voice.

"On the downstairs sofa, of course. He didn't want to mess up one of the guestrooms."

Elli didn't respond, which wasn't like her.

"Why'd you want to know?"

"I thought he might have slept with you. I thought you might have reconciled."

"Reconciled? With Lars?"

She took her eyes off the road and fixed them on me again.

"Lars wasn't the one I saw leaving your house at o dark hundred when I was taking out the trash. In fact, he was leaving Sofi's."

"What?" Excitement raced through me. "Lars spent the night with Sofi?"

"Probably on her sofa."

Almost certainly on her sofa. I was surprised that my sister had let her ex spend the night there at all.

"Wait a minute," I said, obviously slow on the uptake, "if Lars was at Sofi's, who slept on my sofa? Who fed Larry?"

"Jace Night Wind."

The happiness that surged through me was disturbing on several levels, and I tried to analyze it. It was okay to be relieved that he hadn't spent the night with Sonya. It wasn't okay to be pleased that he'd worried enough about me to come back to babysit. I sucked in some deep breaths and made a conscious effort to unclench my fingers.

"He probably just needed a place to sleep. I didn't know he was there."

"Okay. Lars probably just needed a place to sleep, too. Too bad there's not a B and B anywhere nearby."

Jussi & Jussi were quartered in a two-story house-turned-office on Quincy Street in Hancock. It was built of brick, had the steeply pitched roof and was fronted by a closed-in front porch, a feature that had been in fashion when the home was built in the 1930s. It was on the high side of the sloped street, which meant we had to climb up two sets of steep concrete steps to reach it.

"What do the Jussis do if they have an elderly client?"

"They make house calls, of course."

I laughed. "This is probably the last place in the civilized world where lawyers provide that kind of service," I said, thinking of the high-powered, charge-by-the-minute lawyers I'd met in D.C. Elli paused and looked at me.

"At least you're calling us 'civilized.' Remember how badly you wanted to get away from here and have an adventure?"

I'd all but forgotten my youthful restlessness. I had gotten away, but I'd come back home quick enough, my tail between my legs.

The reception area had obviously started life as someone's parlor. There was an arched brick fireplace behind the solid, walnut desk and imposing, leather-covered desk chair, and there were frilly curtains on the windows. The room was unoccupied, but, almost as soon as we arrived, a dapper elderly man opened the glass doors that led to the staircase. He was small and wiry with a full head of wavy white hair. He wore a forest-green plaid shirt, a barn-red tie, a chocolate corduroy sports jacket and a pair of designer jeans. The blue eyes set in the wrinkled face revealed humor and intelligence and a touch of friskiness.

"Hatti, this is Jaakonpoika Jussi," Elli said, as he captured her hand and kissed it. "Jake, this is Hatti Lehtinen." He turned to me and took my hand in his, pressing it, rather than kissing it. Very proper.

"The reigning Red Jacket police chief," he murmured, revealing that he knew the purpose of the visit. "I hope you don't mind walking to lunch."

Only a narrow path had been shoveled on the sidewalk, but, even so, Jake Jussi managed to keep us together by holding Elli's arm with his left hand and mine with his right. I got the impression he'd had plenty of practice squiring ladies. We reached the Kalevala Café in about ten minutes.

"Jake's home away from home," Elli explained, as he deftly held the door for both of us.

"You eat at the same place every day?"

"Not only the same place, he eats the same lunch every day," Elli said, with a laugh. "*Pannakku* with thimbleberry sauce. And coffee."

Jake Jussi winked at me. "Sometimes I order maple syrup just to shake things up."

We were warmly welcomed and assigned the pride of place, a square table near the front window from which we commanded an excellent view of the Christmas wreath on the front of the Miner's Bank across the street and of the business people and Christmas shoppers on the sidewalk.

The pancakes were as good as Elli's, and I found myself wolfing them down.

"I can't believe how good these taste," I mumbled.

Elli smiled at Jake Jussi. "She skipped supper last night and, I suspect, breakfast this morning."

I realized to my astonishment that it was true. It was most unlike me to miss a meal. I was letting the murder case get to me. Or, maybe it was the presence in town of my almost-ex. I set down my fork and took a bracing sip of coffee. I'd be glad when this was all over and things returned to normal.

"I assume," Mr. Jussi said, when we'd finished, "you want to know about Liisa Pelonen."

"That's right," I said. "We understand there was a pretty hefty trust fund coming to her from her mother."

"The trust fund?" He sounded surprised, as if it wasn't the question he'd expected. "Yes, yes, there is a trust fund, as you say, from her mother. She was to get that when she turned twenty-one or when she married, whichever came first." He waited for my next question.

I nodded. "If she had died before Jalmer Pelonen, would he have inherited her money?"

"Yes. As far as I know there is no other immediate relative. Not that he would have needed it, you know. Jalmer had a good deal of money himself."

I was surprised, but not shocked. After all, someone must have paid for Jalmer's elaborate computer setup.

"How much is a 'good deal'?" Elli asked.

"Millions," the attorney said. "Probably six or seven."

"Six or seven million dollars!" Elli and I stared at him, and I wasn't sure which of us had repeated the figure. It was a lot of money anywhere in the country, but on the Keweenaw, it was a fortune.

"He invented an 'App' for the cell phone." Jussi shook his head. "Don't ask me what it does. Don't even ask me what it is."

"But if Jalmer Pelonen had so much money, why did Liisa have to live with the Makis?" Elli asked, reasonably. "Why didn't her father just buy her a car?"

Jake Jussi smiled at her. "He wasn't a spender. Jalmer was a hoarder. He was, however, very fond of his daughter, and I imagine he offered to buy her a car. I believe she wanted to live in Red Jacket, and that caused a rift between them. As far as I know, they had not seen one another since she moved out."

I shook my head. None of this made sense. If Liisa had been frightened of something in Red Jacket, couldn't she have just called on her father for help? He'd had the resources to send her wherever she wanted to go.

"The thing is, Jake," Elli said, "we think the two deaths are linked."

"How? Jalmer died in a car accident, while his daughter had some kind of a heart attack."

I sent Elli a fierce glance. Jake Jussi was probably above suspicion, but I'd thought the same thing about everyone in Red Jacket. Elli got the message.

"Doc Laitimaki isn't certain about Liisa's death," she said, vaguely. "I guess there is some question about whether it could have been foul play."

The lawyer nodded. "There always is a question when money is involved."

That reminded me. "Who inherits the money now?"

"I don't know. We shall have to run a search to see if we can find any family, however remote. If no one turns up, the money will go to the state."

"It's too bad it can't just go to the Keweenaw," Elli muttered. "We could use it. But as it happens, there is a closer relative." She glanced at me for a moment, but I didn't try to stop her. The lawyer would find out about Reid soon enough.

"Liisa Pelonen got married last Friday, on her eighteenth birthday," Elli said. "If she had lived, she'd have been here yesterday to collect her trust fund money."

Jake Jussi's blue eyes widened. "In that case, it goes to her husband."

My heart sank. "He inherits the trust fund?"

"The trust fund and the rest of it. The lucky dog gets the

whole kit and caboodle."

"I don't know how lucky he is," Elli said. "If Liisa was murdered, he'll spend the rest of his life in a jail cell."

Snow that had accompanied us to Hancock had stopped during our lunch, but as we made our way north on 26, the skies opened up again and released golf ball–sized hail that attacked the SUV like a bat on a children's piñata.

"They say the first settlers of this area were the Paleo-Indians, who walked here from Northern Asia," Elli commented. "On days like this I wonder why they didn't just keep heading south."

The words, coming from my cousin the perennial cockeyed optimist, startled me.

"Want me to drive for awhile?"

She shook her head. We both knew our odds were better with her at the wheel.

"Thanks for setting that luncheon up, by the way. It was useful."

"Things look bad for Reid Night Wind."

"The marriage hadn't been consummated. Maybe it isn't a legal marriage. And, anyway, I seriously doubt whether Reid knew about Jalmer's millions."

"He knew about the trust fund. Two million dollars is a strong motive. And how do you know it wasn't consummated? Liisa was pregnant. She'd been sleeping with someone."

"Not with Reid."

"That what he told you? Why would you believe him? Didn't you say he has a police record?"

I flinched. I'd forgotten about that.

"He seems sincere. And his grandfather is a shaman." But he had admitted to Jace and me that he'd married Liisa, in part, because she'd promised him some money. The noose was tightening around Reid's neck. I didn't see any way to save him except to identify the real killer.

"Either he did it or he's being set up," Elli said, her logical mind sorting things out. "Who knew about his relationship with Liisa?"

"Arvo," I said, reluctantly. "Pops."

"Pops is out for obvious reasons."

"It wasn't Arvo," I said. "Remember when he used to play *Joulu pukki* for us?"

"I imagine there are other men who've played Santa Claus who've gone on to kill."

"Elli!"

"No, let me play devil's advocate. We have to figure this out."

"Arvo loved Liisa. He and Pauline both. I think they realized, for the first time, what they'd missed by not becoming parents. They adored having Liisa in the house."

"Maybe it was too much. Maybe having Liisa around made them bitter about what they'd missed."

"El, we're talking about Pops's best friend, a man we've known all our lives. He's not a murderer."

"He might have become one." She looked away from the scattershot of hail against the windshield, and I saw the cynicism in her blue eyes. It was that expression that told me, better than anything else, how much had gone wrong in our insular world.

Suddenly I thought of the dream catcher.

"Listen, El, if Arvo had wanted to frame Reid, he'd have told Sheriff Clump about the dream catcher. As it was, Clump had to ask him about it."

"So Arvo comes off looking innocent. That could have been part of the plot."

I shook my head. "Pauline would have had to be in on it, too."

"Why not? Those two have always been a well-oiled unit. I don't think there's much she wouldn't do for him, and he's devoted to her. Why shouldn't they be in it together?"

I felt a ripple of helpless frustration. "But where's the motive? If they were sick of Liisa–which they weren't–they could have told her to move out. And there's no financial motive. They wouldn't have gotten any of her money or Jalmer's."

"Unless there's another will."

My heart jerked. Another will would put Reid out of danger, but if it left everything to Arvo, he'd be finished.

"Maybe it was Diane Hakala or Barb," I said, grasping at straws. "Maybe it was Ronja."

The SUV hit a patch of black ice, and Elli gripped the steering wheel hard. We hydroplaned, revolved in mid-air and landed facing the wrong way. By the time Elli had steered us out of danger, we'd lost the thread of the debate. I didn't try to pick it up. I was just too glad to be alive.

Elli finally pulled into the old carriage house that served as her garage, and we both collapsed against the seats. After awhile she spoke.

"Have you got a pair of addi-turbos, size six? I need it for a new pattern I'm trying."

I stared at her uncomprehendingly for a long minute.

"Addi-turbos, Hatti," she said. "Knitting needles. I think you've been away from the shop for too long."

My phone rang, and I answered.

"Where are you? Arvo's making tomorrow's memorial service into a double header so he can bury Jalmer and Liisa at the same time. I've got twice as many flower arrangements to make, and you owe me." She was talking about the yellow roses I'd failed to deliver yesterday.

"You're absolutely right. We're on our way."

"Who's we?" My sister sounded both frantic and suspicious, and I was glad to be able to tell her what she wanted to hear.

"Elli Risto."

"Halleluja," Sofi yodeled and hung up.

"Think we should ask her about last night?" Elli asked, as she pulled the SUV back out of the carriage house.

I shook my head. "If there's anything to it, we'll find out eventually."

"That's true. Just like with you and Jace."

I'd never seen Main Street Floral & Fudge so busy. It resembled Grand Central Station at rush hour. I realized, as we wended our way through the throng of fudge-eating customers, it wasn't just because of the double funeral. Folks had gathered to discuss all the news in town, from the deaths of the two Pelonens to the interesting fact that Sofi and I had slept under the same roofs as our husbands last night. I thought I could imagine which topic generated the most interest. I had to fend off several determined attempts to get answers before Elli and I reached the workroom.

Elli slipped on one of Sofi's dark green aprons embellished with a single rosebud and immediately began to work on an evergreen centerpiece.

"The double funeral wouldn't be so bad if it weren't for Christmas," Sofi said, wiping the sweat off her forehead with the back of one hand. "I wish we could just cancel the holiday."

I caught Elli's eye and shook my head. My sister sounded like Snow White's Grumpy. Lars might have spent the night at Sofi's, but there'd been no reconciliation. She did look as though she'd gotten little sleep. There were deep purple crescents under her eyes, and her face was puffy. Maybe they'd stayed up and argued. Geez Louise, I'd be grateful for that. At least it would mean they were talking.

"What do you want me to do?" I asked, although I knew. Sofi pointed to the completed arrangements of snapdragons, daisy poms, glads, greenbills, bachelor buttons and lilies, as well as a box filled with yellow roses. "Take those up to Pauline, would you? Along with the three dozen yellow roses."

I didn't really mind. It'd be a bear driving over in the snowstorm, but once I got there I could snoop around. I knew the Makis were not responsible for the tragedies, but there might be clues somewhere in the house where Liisa had spent her last months of life. I still felt as if I didn't really understand the girl.

The snow was still falling as I eased my way up Main Street in Sofi's van, but it had turned into the fat, wet flakes that are perfect for building snowmen and making snow angels. I finally turned down the alley that ran behind Calumet Street and into the circular drive at the funeral home.

Arvo must have heard me coming, because, by the time I'd parked under the carport and popped open the back, he'd come out to help carry the flowers. We put the first batch in the chapel where Liisa Pelonen, dressed in a simple gown of white wool, rested while the cosmetic floodlights in the pair of torchieres made her look as if she were only sleeping.

I looked at the perfect features and the still body.

"She looks like an angel," Arvo said, fondly.

She is an angel, I thought. Literally. I stared at her dead face. *Who did this to you, Liisa? And why?* I felt a surge of anger, and, at least for that moment, I didn't care whether the killer was Reid or Arvo or anyone else I knew or cared about. I wasn't letting whomever it was get away with it.

We made several trips, and then there were only the yellow roses to be delivered to Pauline for the grave blanket. A phone call summoned Arvo to the interstate, where someone was stranded in the storm. It was a request that came in at least once with every storm, since the hearse was the heaviest vehicle in town, and Arvo never refused.

"I won't be long," he said. "Just take the flowers up to Pauly. She's in the greenhouse."

I took my time walking through the ground floor to the

kitchen, then out to the greenhouse. I considered asking to see Liisa's room again, but there didn't seem much point. Even two days ago it had seemed generic, as if it hadn't belonged to anyone in particular. I wondered who had taken the suitcase. But maybe there wasn't a suitcase. I only had Reid's word for it that she was planning to run away with him. Maybe she'd never intended to go. Maybe she'd never expressed fear of anyone or anything in Red Jacket.

On the other hand, something had threatened her.

I finally entered the conservatory and walked over to the worktable. As always, the place smelled of peat and soil and flowers. It was a restful place, or it should have been, if I hadn't been so agitated by seeing that young body. I laid the roses on the worktable and looked around. Pauline wasn't there.

I waited for awhile. Maybe if I could get Pauline talking about Liisa, she'd remember something that would help. A few minutes later Pauline came into the room using the same door I'd used. I felt like an intruder when she looked startled, but she quickly recovered and thanked me for the roses. I got a sense that she wanted me to leave, but I'd decided I wasn't leaving until I got some answers. The trouble was, I didn't really know the questions. I did, however, have to provide some sort of excuse for invading Pauline's privacy.

"Have you always loved flowers?"

"I studied botany at school," she said, separating the stems with practiced hands. "I got interested in the idea of creating the hybrids, as I told you before."

I nodded. It was a creative activity. Was it also an attempt to control—and manipulate—the environment? I shook off the thought. I was here to find out about Liisa.

"Pauline, was there anything missing in Liisa's room?"

"Missing?"

"Nightgowns, underwear, shoes. Any of her clothes or makeup?"

"I don't think so. Why?"

"Reid Night Wind says he was supposed to meet her in the sauna. They were going to Marquette to live."

Pauline looked at me, her pale eyes amused. "Is that what he told you? It isn't the truth. She wouldn't have gone without telling us, and I don't believe she was in love with anyone."

I considered telling her about the wedding in l'Anse, but I didn't. Pauline didn't need to be hurt any more.

"Did you have a greenhouse before you were married?"

She shook her head. "I always wanted one. Arvo gave it to me for our fifth wedding anniversary."

"That's quite a gift." Or had it been an attempt at compensation because there had been no children?

She began to lay out the yellow roses for the grave blanket. I noticed the bucket of blue gentians nearby.

"Yellow and blue," she said. "Finnish death and Finnish life. I think they'll go well together, don't you?"

CHAPTER SIXTEEN

I stopped back at the house to check on Larry. As expected, the larder was full. There were Jell-O and bean salads in the fridge, along with containers of soups and stew. A blueberry pie sat on the countertop next to a loaf of pumpkin bread and a basket of fresh homemade rolls wrapped up in tin foil. A plate of molasses cookies sat on the table next to a *tiikerikakku*. The tiger cake was created by marbling orange and chocolate layers and frosting it with chocolate fudge. I grinned. It was Pops's favorite.

Sofi, Elli and Charlie showed up for supper and knitting. I didn't ask about Sonya, and I realized with some disgust I was afraid to find out why she hadn't come. After supper we sat in the parlor and worked on individual squares that would eventually be sewn together in an afghan for Mrs. Ryyanen, an elderly lady whose home suffered from a draft. I felt soothed by the clicking of the needles, the feel of the yarn, the satisfaction of completing an inch and then another inch. Knitting, especially knitting with friends, was therapeutic, like working in a greenhouse. I hadn't realized how much I'd missed it during the past four days. I felt almost normal again.

"I called Sonya," Elli said, coming back into the room with fresh mugs of coffee. "She sends her apologies, but she'll be here later. She had to go back down to Houghton to pick up her patient."

Accompanied, I had no doubt, by her gallant knight. My pleasure in the knitting circle evaporated.

Sonya arrived half an hour later, and, to my annoyance, she brought two guests: Jace Night Wind and his brother.

I gritted my teeth as she introduced her new friend, my brother-in-law, around the room, but I forgot all about my irritation when I caught a glimpse of Charlie's face. There were bright red roses in her cheeks, and her pupils were dilated. She looked as if her fairy godmother had just granted her heart's desire. It was the look of love at first sight, impossible to misread. I glanced at Sofi, whose pallor told me she'd seen it, too. I stifled a groan.

Elli filled in the awkward silence.

"How's Cindy Gray Squirrel?"

"Healthy, happy and back home." Sonya touched Jace's shoulder. "She named the baby Jason."

"I hope it was a boy," I muttered under my breath, but my husband heard me. His eyes narrowed on me in an expression I couldn't read. Not that I tried very hard. I wasn't even angry at him. I hated the bone rattling jealousy I felt toward my friend.

I found it impossible to knit under the circumstances, and apparently everyone else did, too, because we just sat around, drank coffee and talked for awhile. Sofi was useless, distracted by worry for her daughter. Charlie was totally focused on the handsome young man who sat cross-legged on the floor beside her. Elli and Sonya tried to carry on a conversation, but it was stilted and awkward, and I felt nothing but relief when Sonya said it was time to go home. Nothing but relief and jealousy.

I bussed the dishes out to the kitchen, then stayed to let Larry out. Sofi came to tell me that Elli had invited the Night Wind brothers to stay at the inn, so she'd left with Reid, while Jace had taken Sonya home.

"I'm leaving now with Charlie," my sister said. She gave me a wan smile.

On the whole, I was glad the day was nearly over. I started

up the front hall staircase when the doorbell rang. I froze, imagining it was the murderer. A fist pounded on the door.

"I know you're in there, Hatti. I can see your shadow through the sidelights. Let me in."

I padded back down the stairs and wrenched open the door.

"What," I asked, "do you want? It's time for bed."

The gray eyes held mine.

"Exactly. And I need one."

"Go next door. Elli's got nothing but beds."

"I'm not married to Elli. I'm married to you, and I think that entitles me to a bed in your house. Or at least a couch."

I didn't think I could sleep knowing he was in the house, so I argued with him.

"Why do you have to sleep here?"

"Because, my lamb, you are alone, and there's a wolf out there somewhere. Do you understand?"

I did. He thought I needed protection. It was nothing personal.

"Fine." I hauled the bedding out of the downstairs closet and handed it to him. "See you in the morning."

It was still dark when something woke me. Not Betty Ann Pritula. I checked the clock and found it was only three A.M., so I fell back onto the bed, closed my eyes and hoped that whatever I'd heard would just go away. It didn't, and the next time I heard it, seconds later, I realized what it was. Barking. And not generic barking, either. It was Larry. I recognized the distinctive baying.

Well, shoot-a-mile. I thrust my feet into the bunnies I'd had since freshman year, looked around for a robe, didn't find one, then hurried down the stairs, my arms wrapped around my T-shirt in a futile attempt to stay warm. I grabbed my parka out of the closet and flung it over my shoulders as I headed toward the kitchen and the back door. That was when I slammed into a large, solid, immovable object whose arms surrounded me, momentarily enveloping me with warmth and a sense of deep security. I realized who it was, though, and started to squawk. Jace slammed my face against the muscles of his chest.

"Hush. Someone's in the backyard."

I jerked my head back to hiss up at him. "I know. It's Larry. Someone left him out."

"Unless Larry has suddenly developed opposing thumbs, he didn't get out by himself."

"What're you saying, Jace?"

"Someone let him out. On purpose."

"Why?" He shushed me again. "Why," I asked, in a whisper. "Just to freak us out?"

"I think the reason's more straightforward than that," he whispered back. "I think someone wants to lure you into the backyard."

I pushed away from him. "Well, he's succeeded. I'm definitely going out there to get my dog."

"Not on foot."

"I'll take the Jeep. He sounds like he's a couple of streets away."

He looked down at my feet. "We'll take the truck. You can't work the clutch in those bunnies."

I nodded. We were wasting time arguing. Jace's theory might be right, but I wasn't convinced that whoever it was didn't intend to send me a warning, like a bassett hound's head in my bed.

On our way through the kitchen, I grabbed Pops's LED Maglite out of one drawer and a knife out of another.

"Put that back," Jace snapped.

"I might need it."

"Only if you're planning to amputate a limb. That's a cleaver."

I didn't want to waste any more time. I dropped the knife on the counter, handed him the flashlight, followed him out the door and down the path I kept shoveled for Larry. The storm had finally stopped. A nearly full moon shone through the lacy clouds and reflected off the smooth mounds of fresh snow. It was like being in the middle of a moonscape, and, under other circumstances, it would have felt magical. Not tonight. I was too worried about Larry.

"Look," I hissed, pointing out the open gate. "Somebody deliberately let him out."

Jace said nothing. He just unlocked the passenger's side door, boosted me into the seat and rounded the truck's hood to get into the driver's side. I automatically buckled my seatbelt while I waited for him. I was anxious to get started when I heard his yell.

"Get out of the truck!"

I responded to the urgency in his voice by trying to fling myself off my seat, but I'd forgotten about the belt. I clawed at it, fear rising in my throat, and then he was there, ripping the metal buckle apart, grabbing me and flinging me, facedown, into the five-foot bank of crusted snow behind the Ikolas' sauna. I tried to lift my head as a hundred and eighty pounds of male landed on my back and drove me into the ground. Snow filled every orifice, and panic slammed into me as I heard a harsh curse and the world exploded.

I pulled off the oxygen mask. I hadn't really needed it. I hadn't been burned in the truck fire, and, thanks, in part, to my burial in snow, I hadn't inhaled too much smoke, either. I stumbled to my feet and wobbled over to observe as medication was applied to the red, puckered splotches on the wide tanned shoulders and back.

"That looks like it hurts," I said to Arne Wierikko, my senior prom date and Red Jacket's sole paramedic.

Arne grunted, not looking at me. He continued to apply salve to the blisters. "Dude's got balls."

I remembered why my mom hadn't liked Arne. And why I had.

"It's fortunate he was wearing a thick leather jacket," said Pauline Maki.

I hadn't known she was in the room. Belatedly, I realized that Pauline, Sofi and Elli were preparing sandwiches and coffee for the firefighters.

"It's really lucky he landed on Hatti," Elli said.

"Yup," Arne agreed. "She woulda been toast."

"What happened exactly?"

Everyone looked at me.

"Jace's truck exploded," Sofi said. "It burst into flames and burned up."

"It caught on the Ikolas' sauna, too," Elli said. "It's a good thing it wasn't connected to their house."

I recalled the horrendous roar and the feelings of panic and imminent suffocation. I remembered the shock of having my face pressed into the snow. I tried to remember what had led up to the violent event. Suddenly, it came to me.

"Larry! Where's Larry?"

"Here." The even note in Jace's voice calmed me. My eyes fixed on him, then slid down to the floor, where Larry reposed, Jace's fingers working behind his ears. I dropped to my knees to embrace the hound and felt tears start behind my eyes.

"He was outside," Jace said, gently. "We heard him bark and went out to find him."

"Someone must have let him out," Pauline put in. "I found him on the back porch when the fire truck arrived."

I knew I should thank my neighbor for bringing him home, but all I could think about was how close we'd all come to incineration.

"Why did the truck explode?" I asked, not releasing my death grip on Larry. I was pretty sure I knew the answer before Jace replied.

"Max Guthrie found a sticky bomb under a fender."

Just like Lars had found a bomb at the scene of Jalmer's death. I flashed back to Jace ripping me out of the seatbelt and tossing me into the snow.

"How did you know there was a bomb?"

I must have sounded suspicious, because the women all turned to look at me, and Arne didn't mince words.

"Thank your stars he figured it out, Hatti. He saved your life."

"I didn't know," Jace said. "Several things were wrong. I'd already figured someone let the dog out to lure you outside, but there was no attack while we crossed the backyard. The other truck bombing must have been in my mind. I felt uneasy as soon as I shut the passenger door, but it took me a coupla more seconds to figure out why."

"Someone wanted to blow me up, but not you?"

The name of Reid Night Wind flitted through my brain.

"I don't think it mattered much to the bomber whether he killed you or me. I think it was meant as a warning."

"Hatti," Pauline said, "you have to take this very seriously. It's time to let the sheriff take over the investigation."

"I agree with Pauline," Sofi said. "We can't have bombs going off all over the place. Anybody could get hurt." I knew she was thinking of Charlie, and I couldn't blame her.

"No." Elli didn't often put her foot down, but when she did, she was immovable. "We've got him on the run now. We can't quit."

I nodded, getting to my feet. "El's right." I tried to think through what my gut was telling me. "Assuming the same person is responsible for everything that's happened, he or she is starting to panic. The snowmobile attack was relatively low risk. So was the bombing of Jalmer's truck. Liisa's murder, if it was murder, was a much bolder stroke that involved cunning and finesse. This truck bombing wasn't clever at all, just desperate. We must be getting close."

The back door opened, and Max Guthrie, volunteer fire chief, stepped onto the mat just inside the door.

"I won't come any farther," he said. "I'm an ashtray. I just wanted to make sure you were all right. You didn't look so hot when Arne and Lars carried you in here on a stretcher." He looked at Jace. "Neither did you, Galahad."

"Galahad?"

Max grinned at me. "The man delivered a baby and saved your life all in twenty-four hours. You should probably marry him."

"Or Sonya should."

The words were out of my mouth before I could think. I was embarrassed and ashamed, but they shut Max up. Everybody but Jace froze.

"If it's not too much to ask," he said, dryly, "could you stop talking about me as if I weren't here?"

After a minute Max spoke again, this time to Jace.

"You were right about the Jeep. How'd you know?"

My husband's face darkened, and his eyes narrowed. "Damn."

I looked from one to the other. "There's a bomb in the Jeep?"

"I told you, Hatti." Jace's voice was rough. "They want to scare you off. From now on you don't take a step outside the house without an escort, you hear me?" He looked at Larry. "You, either, pal."

CHAPTER SEVENTEEN

I stood in the shower in the master bedroom for a long time. I knew I needed to figure out where we were in the investigation, and I needed to get some perspective on my marriage, but I tucked both matters into an invisible compartment and stood still as the water from the showerhead needled against my skin. It was warm and comforting, and there was a great temptation to go to sleep like a cow standing out in a sun-warmed field.

When I felt myself turning into a prune I turned off the shower, rubbed a towel through my hair, then rabbited back across the hall to my own room. My lack of clean clothes reminded me I still hadn't done any laundry, and my folks were due back today. I finally settled on a pair of jeans with rhinestone hearts on the pockets that I'd bought in high school and the white-collared regulation polo shirt we'd been compelled to wear in P.E. Embroidered over the pocket were the words: *Copper County Middle School.*

The housework awaited, but I decided to take a few minutes to write down some notes, so I rummaged in my closet for a half-used notebook and located a pen in my bedside table. I propped the pillows up against the headboard, leaned back and tried to focus on the investigation. Once I figured out who had killed Liisa and Jalmer Pelonen, my marriage would resolve itself. Jace would leave town. I'd be able to proceed with the long-distance divorce without the distraction of those penetrating gray eyes.

I was still propped against the pillows, my unused pen poised, when the door opened, and I felt, again, the full force of those gray eyes. His hair was wet and shone like a raven's wing. Had he showered, too? Where? And he was wearing clean jeans and a red flannel shirt. I'd seen that shirt before, but it had never stopped my breath.

"You borrowed clothes from Max?"

His grin was slow and so familiar. "I like that shirt. Kind of has the school-girl fantasy vibe going for it. Let me guess, it's laundry day."

His friendliness, so unexpected, disarmed me, and I didn't object when he shoved me over to make room for himself against the bank of pillows. He dropped his head back, his long lashes closed over the disturbing eyes, but only for a minute.

"What's that on the ceiling?"

"Glow-in-the-dark stars. My dad and I put them up during an astronomy unit in the second grade."

"Your stepdad," he said, but his tone was mild, and he closed his eyes again while he yawned. I gazed at the face next to mine on the pillow.

"He's coming home today, with my mom. I'd like you to meet him."

"I doubt I'll have a choice."

There was no bite behind the comment, but it showed me where I stood. Of course he didn't want to meet my father. We were about to divorce. When the pain began to pass, I finally realized something about Jace, something that had probably had a major impact on our brief marriage.

"This hostility about fathers is really about your own, isn't it?"

I could see his lips tighten, but he answered me civilly enough.

"I have no feelings one way or the other for my own father.

185

I've never met him." His eyes opened, and suddenly he was all business. "Look, we've got to figure out what the hell's going on here."

"That's what I intended to do," I said, determined to be as businesslike as he. "I just don't know where to start."

"Start with this." He moved like chain lightning, canting up on one elbow, leaning over me and kissing me hard on my chapped lips. The kiss ended as abruptly as it had begun, and he settled back against the pillows. "Thought that might get your juices flowing."

I gaped at him. *What the hell was that?*

"Close your mouth. You look like a codfish. C'mon, let's get to work."

"I'll start with the suspect list," I said, my voice a little shaky. I wrote down two names: *Ronja Laplander, Diane Hakala.*

"This isn't a game, Umlaut. This is a real and present danger. It's time to cut to the chase. Those women might have resented Liisa Pelonen, but they had no reason to kill her father. The motive is in the money. It has to be."

"That leaves Reid."

"Not necessarily."

"Think about it, Jace. He admits he married Liisa to get money from her trust fund. He had a rendezvous set up with her just about the time the murder took place. Let's assume Liisa had told him about her father's wealth and he figured out that if he got rid of her, he'd be set up for life. He's got experience with chemicals from his days with the cat lab, and he's got access to herbs, some of them poisonous, through his grandfather, a shaman. Even if we find out she was poisoned, he's the most obvious suspect. Clump knows about the dream catcher, and he's not a fool. He's probably put two and two together. I'm surprised he hasn't already arrested Reid."

Jace's face was twisted into a frown.

"Maki did it," he said, as if I hadn't just laid out a great case against his brother. "I've just got to figure out how he gets the money."

I shook my head. "I'm sorry about Reid, but we can't pin this on Arvo even if we want to. There's no way he'd inherit. Without an heir the fortune would go to the state, but, unfortunately, there is an heir."

"Thank you," he said. My eyes widened.

"For what?"

"For using the word 'we.' "

"Aunt Hatti! Aunt Hatti!" the door burst open, and Charlie catapulted into the room. She raced over to the bed and grabbed my arm, heedless of the fact that I was not alone. "The sheriff's here. He's come to arrest Reid. Aunt Hatti, he says you called him!"

Jace removed himself from the bed in one graceful move. The look he lasered at me could have curdled milk.

"Judge, jury and executioner," he said, softly. "Whatever it takes to save your Grand Pooh Bah."

I didn't bother to defend myself. If Jace believed I would turn Reid in behind his back there was nothing I could do about it. I got to my feet and trailed the other two down the stairs. At least one thing was certain.

My marriage was truly over.

CHAPTER EIGHTEEN

Horace Clump had been sheriff of Copper County for as long as anyone could remember, certainly long enough to be referred to as a "valued institution" or a "favorite son." He was called neither.

He was fifty years old and egg-shaped. His walk had become a waddle, and he hadn't worn a belt since the turn of the century. These days his brown uniform pants with the stripe on the outsides were held up by a pair of bright red suspenders that he'd taken to snapping with his thumbs. His shaven head always reminded me of a bullet. It did nothing to offset the sagging jowls or the liver-colored loose lips.

Clump's lack of physical beauty was not why he was disliked. No one liked him, with the possible exception of his thin-lipped wife, RaeAnne, and his three surprisingly pretty daughters. He was physically lazy but ambitious, and he'd been methodically consolidating his power by pressuring small communities, like ours, to sign contracts with him for law enforcement services. One of the reasons I'd agreed to the temporary policing job was to prevent the takeover, to save Pops's position as Red Jacket police chief.

I tried to hide my dislike, which I knew was unfair. Before today I'd never had any personal dealings with the man. Now he was in my kitchen, sprawled in the chair Jace had sat in the night after the murder, and he hadn't bothered to take off his hat. He didn't stand up, either. I thought about how disgusted my mother would be at this flouting of manners.

"Good morning, sheriff. Would you like some coffee?"

"Yer sister's takin' care of that, Hatti."

His tone wasn't hostile, but by using my first name he was putting me firmly in my place. I was to be treated like a kid, not a law enforcement equal.

"This here's Elwood Snow," he said, jerking his thumb, hitchhiker-like, at the tall, thin individual who had risen from the table. "Elwood's my latest deputy." He pronounced it "depooty." Elwood must be the latest in a revolving door of deputies, a position Lars had once held for several years. Like I said, no one can tolerate Clump for very long.

I glanced at Sofi, who was filling mugs with fresh, fragrant coffee. Finns always offered visitors coffee. My mother would prepare coffee for a burglar.

"I'm here to collect Reid Night Wind. I'd 'ppreciate it if you'd call 'im."

I ignored the request. "I don't know if you've met Reid's brother, Jason Night Wind," I said. "He's Chief Joseph's grandson and a lawyer from Washington, D.C."

Clump undoubtedly knew all that. At any rate, he wasn't impressed.

"I know 'im," he said, with a glint in the dark half-moons that were his eyes. "We've had some truck about this boy before." I winced, inwardly, remembering Reid's other brushes with the law.

"Sheriff," Jace said, with cold courtesy, "I'd like to see your warrant."

Clump sniggered. "Ain't got one. Just wanna have a little chat with the rascal."

I wasn't fooled by the Andy Griffith-routine, and I knew Jace wasn't either, but we both knew Clump was within his rights to question Reid.

"Ain't got a warrant for you, either, Hatti, but sometime I'd like to have a little sit-down. You shoulda called me as soon as the corpse turned up."

I knew he was right. But I knew, too, that Arvo had been right. Clump would have reduced Liisa Pelonen to a statistic, just as he was doing now. I wasn't sorry I'd tried to investigate. I was only sorry I had failed.

"No hurry on that now," Clump drawled. "I got the pitcher."

He was convinced of Reid's guilt just as Jace was convinced of my betrayal. I heard the scorn in Clump's voice and saw it in Jace's eyes.

"This here's gonna be a slam dunk."

I heard an anguished sob and realized Charlie was in the kitchen, too, down on the floor with Larry.

"I'm afraid I don't know what you mean," I said, maintaining my dignity as much as it was possible to do in the circumstances. "I wasn't aware there was any proof."

I knew I'd said the wrong thing the instant the words were out of my mouth. Jace was holding a mug of coffee, and I watched his knuckles turn white.

Sheriff Clump chortled and snapped his fingers at Elwood. The deputy dug into his pocket and pulled out a much-folded square of paper. The sheriff scowled at him.

"Dad gummit, boy, why'd you have to wrinkle it up?"

The deputy was too new at the job to realize he'd be better off not answering the rhetorical question.

"Had to make it fit in my pocket," he mumbled.

"Damn fool." Clump unfolded the paper and held it out to Jace, who stepped forward to take it. "Proof positive yer brother's a murderer."

Fear gripped my heart. "What is it?"

Jace, not surprisingly, didn't answer me. He didn't hand over the paper, either.

"Marriage license," Clump said, triumph in his voice. "Show's that Night Wind married the Pelonen girl on December thirteenth, the day she was to inherit her money. Turned out to be a damned lucky day for him, too. With her dead and her old man, too, he gets the whole enchilada."

I reflected, briefly, that Clump might be the only person on the Keweenaw who'd use a phrase like that. I wondered how he'd gotten ahold of the license. I wondered how in the H-E-double hockey sticks Reid was going to get out of this.

"How'd you get ahold of this, sheriff?"

The question came from Jace. I knew he didn't expect an answer or need one. He thought I'd provided the sheriff with the evidence.

"Don't much matter how, does it?"

The back door opened. Elli entered first, followed by Reid, whose raven hair was still wet from a shower. His dark face glowed with good health. I thought he looked unbearably young and a little scared under his cocky attitude. I heard another little sob from Charlie.

"Lookin' for me, sheriff?"

The fat man heaved himself up from the chair. "I come to offer you some hospitality at the county's expense. You'd best bring a bag. You may be with us for some time."

"You need a warrant to take him in," I said, knowing it was a losing battle.

Clump nodded. At least I thought he nodded. It was hard to tell with no neck.

"I kin get one anytime. I not only got the proof on paper," he nodded at the document still in Jace's hand, "I gotta eyewitness says young Night Wind here was seen outside the Makis' sauna at seven P.M. December thirteenth."

But Reid had said he'd been late getting to the appointment.

"What eyewitness?"

"Neighbor lady named Ikola. Got a signed statement from her."

The Ikola family were our backdoor neighbors. If Grace Ikola had been in the upstairs back bedroom, she'd have been able to see a person in the Makis' yard, even in the snow-filled dark.

"It's okay, Hatti," Reid said, quietly. "I'll go with him. I didn't kill Liisa, and they can't prove I did."

But the evidence was piling up, and it was starting to look irrefutable. Fear for the young man skittered up my spine. Whoever had framed Reid Night Wind had been extremely thorough.

"The autopsy report concludes that Liisa's death was an accident," I said, desperate to halt the juggernaut of doom.

"Hell, girl. You know and I know nobody never died from fainting. There's another reason for the girl's death, and we'll find it. Meantime, this here boy coulda made the bomb that done in Jalmer's car with his eyes closed."

"Anybody could have made it with their eyes closed. There're verbal instructions on You Tube."

Clump had had enough kibbitzing.

"Let's go, boy," he said, apparently to his deputy. "Cuff 'im."

Charlie's sobs turned to wails, and I saw Reid throw her a concerned look.

"I'll be okay," he said, as Elwood snapped the bracelets on him. "Like I said, I didn't do it. Keep the faith."

"I'll be right behind you," Jace told his brother. He made a face as if remembering he no longer had a vehicle. I grabbed the extra keys to the Jeep off the pegboard by the door.

"Take the Jeep."

The gray eyes glinted with humor for a fraction of a second.

"Generous," he said, "considering the bomb."

Silence filled the room after the men had left.

"Hatti." My sister was on one side, my cousin on the other.

"You're as white as a sheet. Why don't you lie down for awhile?"

Elli nodded her head in agreement with Sofi. "We'll call Sonya, and the four of us will put our heads together. How about a one o'clock lunch at Patty's?"

I agreed to the suggestion partly because I wanted to be left alone and partly because I knew my knitting sisters would have good ideas later on. I ushered them out the door, called Doc and made an appointment for later in the morning, then I rushed around the house getting it ready for my returning parents.

At quarter to eleven I shoved my arms into my pink parka, grabbed my purse and headed out the front door. I'd have to borrow the van from Sofi. Once again I found a sexy, male animal prowling around my front porch.

"I came to provide you with company," Max said, obviously concerned for my safety, "that is, if you need it."

"What I really need," I said, "is a ride. Have you got an hour?"

He shrugged and smiled. "Hey, I can be a Galahad, too."

We started the five-mile drive to Frog Creek and Doc's office. The sky was pregnant with snow, and flakes were coming down at an alarming rate. I thought about the funeral this afternoon and my folks on the road from Minnesota. Sometimes living on the Keweenaw was one big pain. I started to fill Max in on the sheriff's visit, but he stopped me. He'd already heard.

A few minutes later we passed the sheriff's office on Lake Superior Street. Were they all still in there? Was Jace trying desperately to come up with a strategy to cut the net in which his brother was caught? Doc's home-slash-office was three blocks farther down on the same street. I told Max to park on the street in front of Doc's door, which he was able to do with his four-wheel drive.

★　★　★　★　★

Doc's place was a depression-era bungalow that looked as if it had been built for elves. The white brick was set off with a swooping roofline, and there was a rickrack of red trim on the door and windows. There was a small window in the top of the door. It reminded me of the window in the wall around the Emerald City. I always expected a gatekeeper to stick his head out and ask my business.

Inside the ceilings were low, and the rooms were small. The amazing thing about the whole set up was that Doc was large, well over six feet and stocky. He had to duck practically every time he moved, but it didn't seem to bother him. Nothing much seemed to bother him as long as Mrs. Doc was happy. And Mrs. Doc, Flossie, loved the little cottage.

Doc greeted us at the door, his bald head shining, his white beard resting on his massive chest.

"*Hei*, Hatti," he said, gathering me into a hug. "This your young man?"

I didn't know what to say, but Max did. He chuckled.

"Been a long time since I was called a 'young man.' "

I introduced the two as Doc took us into his office and offered us chairs. The room was cheerful and cozy, and, with a fire in the grate, it was warm.

"Max owns Namagok." I figured it would be explanation enough. Doc, like everybody else, knew I'd married a half-Ojibwe who was related to Chief Joseph, not some displaced cowboy.

Doc nodded and asked about Sofi and the rest of the family. I asked about Flossie, the children and grandchildren. Amazingly, we finished with the pleasantries in only a few minutes.

Doc leaned back in his chair.

"All right, *tytar.*" I smiled at his use of "daughter" and the fact that I didn't mind. "You want to know what I can tell you about Liisa Pelonen, eh? Well, I'm sorry to say, it isn't much."

"You can't find any indication she was murdered?"

He shook his head.

"Is it possible the fainting was brought on by some kind of poison?"

"I couldn't find anything."

"But what if it was something that wouldn't show up on the screen?"

He shrugged. "I am not an expert, eh? But there was no smell, no blue lips."

I thought of Reid Night Wind down the street in the sheriff's office. I had to try harder to find out who'd really killed Liisa.

"Can you test for other kinds of poisons?"

"Yah. Too many. Hundreds. I need to know what you suspect."

Something about the way he answered gave me hope.

"You suspect something, too."

He rubbed the back of his big neck. "The faint shouldn't have killed her. Not when there was nothing wrong with her heart. Poison would explain it. But which? I don't know."

"It might be easier to guess which poison was used," Max said, "if there was a clear suspect."

I could see his point. The trouble was I didn't like either of the two main suspects. I wanted the villain to be a stranger.

Doc looked intrigued.

"You mean, if the suspect is a doctor or a pharmacist, he might use prescription pills, eh?"

Max nodded. "If he is a gardener, he might use some kind of weed killer."

"But weed killer would leave physical signs, wouldn't it?" I was struggling to understand.

"There are natural killers, too. The leaves and berries of certain plants and flowers are poisonous."

His words recalled my conversation with Pauline in her

greenhouse. Plants, unlike animals who had camouflage and mobility, had nothing to protect them except prickers and poisons. Pauline had poisonous specimens among the rows of brightly colored flowers. And Arvo had access to them.

The silence in the room assured me that Max and Doc had connected the same dots. In my heart I didn't believe it was possible. But in my head? I thanked Doc, and we left. Weather conditions had worsened, making visibility almost nonexistent. Max drove slowly but with confidence.

"When you've eliminated the possible, whatever remains, however improbable, is the truth."

I stared at him.

"Sherlock Holmes," he replied to my unasked question. "A good detective has to apply logic to get to the truth, Hatti. And Holmes was a very good detective."

"You think Arvo Maki is behind this?"

He shrugged. "Look at the facts. Did he have motive? Means? Opportunity?"

I forced myself to really think.

"He was in and out of the B and B that night. He knew Liisa was home alone with a sore throat. He knew about her relationship with Reid Night Wind and may have known about the planned rendezvous." I swallowed. "He had access to poisons from the greenhouse, and he certainly had the strength to clobber her with a sauna rock." I paused. "The thing is, he had no motive. He couldn't have inherited the money."

"Money's not the only motive," Max said, carefully. "How did he feel about Liisa Pelonen?"

"He says he loved her, and I believe him."

"Love is a strong emotion for a girl who is really just a houseguest."

I turned toward him. "You're saying love can make a person vulnerable." He didn't respond. "You think Arvo expected too much from Liisa, and that when she disappointed him, he was so frustrated he killed her."

"It's been known to happen."

"But it wasn't a jealous kind of love."

Max shrugged, his eyes carefully focused on the barely discernible road ahead of us. "Strong emotions of any kind make behavior unpredictable. The majority of violent crime take place between people who know each other. Love of any kind can and does go wrong."

I detected a thread of bitterness in the words and wondered about his past. Was that what had happened to Max? Had a failed love affair driven him north to our secluded peninsula? It was a question for another time. At the moment, I needed to focus on Liisa and her killer.

"You have to ask yourself: Is Arvo smart and calculating enough to have set up a complicated scheme that involved getting rid of the police chief, killing an ice fisherman and his daughter, and rigging the bombs at your place?"

I thought of all the festivals and fundraisers and community events designed to save Red Jacket from disappearing the way the mines had. Arvo had been behind all of them. Looking back it almost seemed as if he'd kept us viable by sheer charisma and the force of his will. He'd had help, of course, from Pauline and all the rest of us. Red Jacket was our home, and we loved it almost as much as he did. Almost as much. Arvo Maki was a man of strong emotions. I hadn't thought of him in quite that way before.

"Let me buy you lunch," Max said, when we'd reached the edge of town. "It's almost one."

I'd nearly forgotten my plans to meet Sofi, Elli and Sonya. I explained to Max and invited him to join us. He declined but parked and came inside with me, saying he'd pick up lunch to go. I got the feeling he did it just to make sure I didn't get blown up or bopped on the head with a sauna rock before I'd met my friends. He greeted Sofi, smiled at Elli and nodded, coolly, at Sonya, who barely acknowledged him. I wondered whether Sofi was right about those two.

Pasties, which are actually pies composed of meat, vegetables and a flaky crust, were invented for the miners in Cornwall because they stayed hot all day. The concept crossed the Atlantic with the immigrants coming to work in the copper and iron mines in the U.P., and the pasty had become iconic on the Keweenaw. Nowadays, though, there are pasties for every taste: vegetarian pasties, salad pasties, tuna, chipotle, Asian pasties, Italian pasties with pasta and, for the fast-food lover, the bacon-cheeseburger pasty. Patty's pasties are all delicious.

Once we'd finally put in our order, Sonya kicked off the pow-wow.

"The case against Reid Night Wind is starting to look water tight. The sheriff knows Reid was married to Liisa, and Elli tells me Reid stands to inherit something like eight million dollars. On top of that, there's an eyewitness that can place Reid in the Makis' backyard at seven P.M. the night of the murder. Jace is worried."

So Jace had contacted Sonya this morning. I tried to ignore the stab of jealousy, but something must have shown on my face. I felt Sonya's gaze on me.

"He called his grandfather. I was out on the rez, and Chief Joseph asked me to take some fresh clothing for Reid since I was coming back this way."

It made sense. It was also nice of Sonya to explain. It didn't make me feel better, though. I'd never formally met Chief Joseph, my father-in-law.

"We only have Reid's word for it that he didn't kill Liisa," Sofi pointed out, "but let's go over the points. I can't see that the eyewitness matters. Reid admits he had a date to meet Liisa at the sauna at seven."

I'd thought about that a little. "I'd like to know how Clump got Grace Ikola's eyewitness account. I mean, we know he didn't send Elwood door to door to ask whether the neighbors had seen anything."

"Grace?" Sonya looked confused. "The Ikola woman's name wasn't Grace. It was something else. A stuttering sort of name."

Elli frowned. "You mean Aaarti?"

"That's it."

"That's absurd," I burst out. "Aaarti is the grandmother."

Elli nodded. "She sits up in that back window most of the day, but there's no way she could have seen Reid or anyone else. She's legally blind."

We exchanged significant glances around the table.

"It sounds to me like someone is trying too hard to frame this kid," Sofi said. I couldn't help feeling a little proud of her. I was sure my sister would be happier if Charlie never saw Jace's hunky younger brother again, but she was, as always except in the case of her own ex, fair-minded.

I frowned. "We still don't know how Clump found out about the dream catcher or the marriage license. Think somebody's feeding him this stuff?"

"Looks like it," Elli said. "The question is, who?"

"I think we should let Jace know his brother has been set up," Sonya put in.

"He knows," I said, wishing I didn't sound as irritated as I felt. "We can help him best by finding out who's behind it." I sucked in a breath and told them about my conversation with Doc. "I think we need to find out what kinds of poisons there are in a greenhouse."

Everyone was silent for a moment. Finally, Elli spoke.

"Do we really think Arvo could have killed that unfortunate girl?"

Sonya's dark blue eyes were filled with sympathy for those of us who'd known the man all our lives.

"It must have been a shock to find out she was pregnant."

"He told me he was happy about that," I said.

"I know." Sonya's smile was gentle. "But if a person can kill, he can lie. You never really know what's going on inside someone else's head. Or heart."

She was right, of course. We were going to have to seriously consider Pops's best friend for this murder.

"There's still Matti Murso," Elli said, but there wasn't much conviction in her voice.

"All right," Sofi said, bracingly. "You're in charge, Hatti. What do you want us to do?"

I gathered my thoughts. "We've got a couple of hours until the funeral. You, Sofi, check your horticultural books and ask Charlie to look up plant poisons on line. Sonya, can you do a little research on medicinal herbs traditionally used on the rez?" I turned to Elli. "Check with Mr. Jussi to see whether he's come up with a next of kin in Jalmer's family."

"What about you?" Sofi asked.

"I'm going to go stand in the shower and let the little gray cells go to work."

CHAPTER NINETEEN

I walked home, up Main Street to Third and then Calumet. The snow was still falling, but it had thinned out. Nevertheless, the streets and yards and rooftops were coated with a thick layer of white icing that made our shabby little town look picturesque.

I wished things hadn't fallen apart between Jace and me. I'd have liked to check in with him to see how Reid was holding up, to offer support and to tell him we were now firmly on the trail of his favorite suspect, Arvo Maki. He wouldn't want to hear from me, though. He'd decided he couldn't trust me. Was that at the root of our marriage's epic fail? Had he decided a year ago that he couldn't trust me? Had something happened during his visit to the Keweenaw in those weeks before Christmas? I'd probably never know.

I didn't go upstairs immediately. I let Larry out into the backyard maze and watched him from the back porch. There were more casserole dishes and plates of baked goods on the countertops. It was good that we'd adopted the milk chute strategy, I thought. It was an efficient way for us to take care of one another. Would that change now that we'd had a murder in our midst?

Larry padded in through the back door, shook the snow off his solid frame and planted himself in front of me for a little ear scratching. I obliged. I figured he deserved some attention, and the repetition of scratching behind the ears might just pitch me into a meditative trance. I needed some help from my subconscious.

"Tell you what," I said, after a few rubs, "let's do this in Pops's study. It's more conducive to deep thinking." The basset hound straightened his stubby back legs, stretched, wagged his tail once, then followed me into the next room. An open book lay facedown on the arm of Pops's upholstered chair. I picked it up, glanced at the title and felt the hair raise on the back of my neck. I sat, and, forgetting all about Larry, I read. When I finally lifted my head, I thought I knew most of the story.

I knew who had killed Liisa Pelonen, and I knew what had killed her. I still didn't know how it was done. Neither did I have any proof. But the clouds had cleared in my mind, leaving a brilliant sky, and written on that sky was the name of my stepfather's closest friend.

I dug my cellphone out of my pocket, punched in Doc's number and told him my deductions. He offered to run a test and get back to me.

For a long moment I stared out at the worsening storm, so the phone was still in my hand when Elli called. She was almost too excited to talk.

"Okay, Hatti, I checked with Jake Jussi. He said he'd called Helsinki, an organization called the Population Information System. It's like a huge bank of information and houses all the vital records of Finns, both those living inside the country and out of it. He found Jalmer."

"Why would Jalmer be in a Finnish data system? He is, I mean he was, an American."

"Exactly," Elli said, triumphantly. "He shouldn't have been in it. Jake said he's listed because of his Finnish wife."

Surely there was nothing significant about that. Finns, especially those of us in the U.P., had taken longer to assimilate than other groups of immigrants.

"You mean Liisa's mother."

"No, no. Liisa's mother died about fifteen years ago. This is another wife. A second wife."

I was speechless.

"Jake managed to locate her. They were paired up by an online matchmaker and married the same way."

I thought about the sophisticated computer system at the cabin in Ahmeek.

"He must have gotten tired of his unibomber-like existence."

"Or," Elli offered, "maybe he just realized he'd need help rearing a teenage girl."

"So he got himself a mail-order bride, but apparently it didn't work out. What's her name?"

"Gearda Ahkebeaivi."

"A Sami. That explains a lot."

The Sami people, also called Laplanders or Lapps, hail from the northernmost reaches of the Scandinavian countries. They are considered indigenous people and, traditionally, have lived semi-nomadic lives as herders of reindeer.

"She was only on the Keweenaw about three weeks. There was a language barrier, of course, and she said she couldn't adjust to the crowds of people and the warm winter weather."

"Poor Jalmer," I said; "poor her."

"She returned to her family and their herding business, but here's the really interesting part: she and Jalmer were never divorced."

I gasped. "So the reindeer wife is Jalmer's heir."

"Jake says she'll get about six million dollars."

"That's a lot of reindeer food. What do they eat, anyway?"

"Plants, I think," Elli said.

Plants.

"This won't get Reid Night Wind off the hook, I'm afraid," Elli went on, following her own train of thought. "He's still in line to inherit Liisa's trust fund, and two million dollars is a powerful enough motive for murder."

"Forget about Reid," I told her. "He didn't do it. But, El, I'm pretty sure I know who did. And how. Or, at least I know what the substance was that killed her. It's called aconite, a kind of poison derived from a beautiful blue flower called wolfsbane or monkshood."

"What makes you think it's aconite?"

"It paralyzes the nerves, lowers blood pressure and stops the heart. Like a faint."

"Did you find it in a book?"

I knew she meant a nonfiction book about poisons.

"It was a mystery by Ellis Peters featuring a medieval monk who is both an herbalist and a detective. It was the name of the book, *Monkshood,* that got me thinking about it. And here's the really weird part. I found the book open to an explanation of the poison. It was just sitting on Pops's chair."

"You hadn't put it there yourself?"

"I don't remember ever seeing it before."

"Spooky. Maybe a *tonttu* put it there."

The *tonttu* were mythical creatures, gnomes with sparkly blue eyes, who lived in homes and protected the people who lived there, too. I thought of my personal *tonttu*, Einar. Had he brought the book?

"It could have been anybody who knew about the key in the milk chute."

"Right."

"Even if you're right, how did the poison get into Liisa's body? And how does that clear Reid Night Wind?"

I heard the unhappiness in her voice and knew she'd guessed the answer to the second part of the question.

"I'm hoping Doc will tell me how it got there. As far as the rest of it, well, I saw the monkshood flowers in Pauline's greenhouse."

"So you think Arvo is the killer?"

"I don't think that, El. I don't want to think it. All we can do is gather facts and hope they'll lead us to the truth."

She was silent for a moment.

"I think it's time to turn this over, Hatti. It's getting too close to home."

By which she meant it was getting too dangerous.

"Soon," I said, soothingly. "I need some proof first." My call-waiting beeper. "That's probably Doc. I'll let you know when there's something to know."

"You nailed it, Henrikki," Doc said, when he came on the line. His voice was heavy and sad. "I found the aconite. How did you guess?"

I decided not to go into the help I'd gotten from Ellis's Brother Cadfael.

"The flowers in Pauline's greenhouse."

"*Joo.* I was afraid of that."

"Doc, where did you find the toxin? I mean, was it in her stomach?"

"*Ei.* She didn't ingest it. And there were no punctures to indicate it went directly to her bloodstream."

"What if I tell you everything I know about that Friday night?"

"*Hyvä.* If you think it would help."

"Liisa caught a chill and complained of a sore throat after the parade. Pauline brought her home, sent her to take a hot shower, bundled her into her nightgown, made her a cup of tea with honey and tucked her into bed. When she returned, about half an hour later, Liisa was sleeping."

"The murderer must have forced the toxin into her system," Doc said. "Perhaps through the skin."

I was thunderstruck. "Oh my gosh! I forgot. Pauline rubbed Vicks on Liisa's chest to help with the congestion."

"Someone may have tampered with the Vicks," he said. "The plant could have been ground into tiny pieces and mixed with it."

"But, if that were true, wouldn't the poison have killed Pauline, too?"

"*Ei.* Pauline is fastidious, you know. She would have scrubbed her hands immediately. The poison would take some minutes to work, too."

"Does that mean Liisa was dead when Pauline checked on her at six forty-five?"

"Most probably."

"Pauline wouldn't have gone all the way over to the bed. She was getting jam for the visitors from Lansing and would have been in a hurry. She'd have thought Liisa was just asleep."

My mind was moving fast now, like a rock picking up speed as it rolled down a hill. I suddenly remembered I'd seen the jar of Vicks on the worktable in Pauline's greenhouse. How simple it would have been for Arvo to slip in there, mix up the fatal potion and leave it in the bathroom assigned to Liisa. He had to know that Pauline was most likely to administer the salve, but it was a fairly small risk. Doc was right about Arvo's wife. She would have washed her hands immediately.

"So, if you are right, Pauline killed the girl, unwittingly."

"Do you think I'm right?"

"I wish I could say no, Henrikki. You need to tell the sheriff."

"I know." But I couldn't tell Clump. Not until I had evidence. A confession would be perfect, but I'd settle for the tainted jar of Vicks.

"This will not be good for the town," Doc said. I knew he was right. Arvo Maki was our sparkplug. It was through his efforts, and those of his wife, that we'd remained viable in an area where businesses had closed and the youth had gone.

I thanked Doc and hung up. I had to find the guts, the *sisu,* to pursue this thing to the end, no matter who got hurt. I couldn't let Reid Night Wind pay for a crime he hadn't committed. I wouldn't.

The funeral was set to start in a little more than an hour. I figured it wouldn't hurt to be just a little early.

I vaulted up the stairs to my room and threw on an ancient knitted dress. Having started life as a tunic, it was inappropriately short, but at least it was black. I snatched a pair of black tights from my mother's dresser, found the knee-high black boots I'd loved in high school but which now made me feel like a dominatrix, and I borrowed my mother's faux fur jacket, which gave me the breadth and texture of a black bear but had the virtue of deep pockets. I was going to need those pockets.

I made a decision about the dream-catcher pendant and slipped it into my pocket. It would make a good excuse if I needed one. Downstairs in the kitchen, almost as an afterthought, I grabbed a little insurance. I put that in my pocket, too. I knew I could do this better by myself, but I wasn't unaware of the danger. I should let someone know.

"Wish me luck," I told Larry. He raised his liquid brown eyes without lifting his head. I leaned down and scratched him behind the ears, remembering, as I did so, Jace's long fingers engaged in the same activity. It came to me that there was one person I could safely contact, one person who would send some kind of backup but who wouldn't show up himself. Jace had made it clear I was no longer his business. I texted him a message, then headed for the showdown.

Unfortunately, the fur jacket did not have a hood, and I'd forgotten to wear a hat. By the time I'd crossed the fifty feet to the Makis' front door, the snow had soaked my hair. I told myself it didn't matter. Today wasn't about looking good.

Today was about catching a murderer.

The door was unlocked, as it always was on funeral days. I recognized the majestic arrangement of yellow lilies, roses and delphiniums in a copper container on the pedestal in the corridor. I recognized the face on the front of the programs stacked on the reception desk. It didn't do justice to Liisa's ethereal, blonde loveliness or to her sky-blue eyes. I could understand Matti's crush, Reid's urge to protect and Arvo's fascination with her. There was, of course, no photo of Jalmer Pelonen. I doubted whether a photo of the hermit existed.

Classical music and soft lights, along with the solid structure of the house, muted the crashing sounds of the storm outside, but I didn't feel safe. Was Arvo in his office? Upstairs getting dressed? Back in the kitchen? On the one hand, I couldn't imagine him hurting me. On the other, well, he'd already killed at least once and more likely twice. I wiped my boots on the mat and started down the corridor. The doors of the office and embalming room were closed, but the chapel was wide open and empty. It was a perfect opportunity to take care of one of my self-imposed tasks. I walked toward the casket on the altar. The golden hair gleamed in the spotlight. I felt a familiar pang as I looked into the young face. Too young to die. I had to remember that if my nerve failed.

I pulled the dream catcher out of my pocket and slipped it under the counterpane pulled up to her waist. Somehow I felt it was right for her to have it. "Rest in peace," I whispered.

There was still no sign of the Makis or anyone else when I re-emerged from the chapel, but I knew folks would start to arrive soon. I had a mission, and it was time to do it. I strode down the corridor through the darkened kitchen and into the greenhouse. Sleet and hail and the occasional roll of thunder made a cacophony of noises that did nothing for my nerves, but the windowed room was brighter than the rest of the gloomy house, and the scents of loam and fertilizer and earth were somehow reassuring. The greenhouse, I thought, not for the first time, with its aura of new life was the perfect antidote to the mortuary.

I was relieved that it, too, was empty. I didn't relish telling Pauline I'd come to collect the evidence that could convict her husband of murder. I hurried down the aisle between plant tables, my eye on the worktable at the back. I failed to notice a clay pot that had gotten dislodged from the neat stacks beneath one of the tables. My toe hit it, triggering an explosion of pain and a muffled curse. When it had subsided a little, I stooped down to replace the pot and found that it wouldn't go. There was some kind of obstruction. I got all the way to my knees, reached under and felt my fingers wrap around a webbed strap of some kind. I gave it a sharp tug and an object as big and almost as heavy as Larry flew out from under the table and landed on my lap. It was a pink backpack.

Hastily I unzipped it and thrust my hand inside. I found frilly underwear, a laptop computer, a wallet and an Ipod. It was more than a backpack. It was Liisa's missing suitcase. She really had intended to run off with Reid. Arvo hadn't been able to face the loss. He'd stopped her the only way he could, and then he'd hid her belongings.

Motive, means and opportunity.

I replaced the backpack and the pot and got to my feet, wishing I felt happier about solving the crime. I could see the little jar of Vicks on the worktable, but, before I reached it, Pauline Maki emerged from the far side of the greenhouse. Her sudden appearance made my heart carom against my ribs. Had she been here the whole time? She was wearing shapeless slacks and an old sweater covered with an apron. Her face was bereft of makeup and her hair untidy.

I asked the first thing that popped into my head.

"Why aren't you ready for the funeral?"

She stared at me, unsmiling, and I saw something in her eyes that reminded me of Miss Irene's verses, not from the King James but from the Book of Common Prayer.

"From envy, hatred, malice, and all uncharitableness, Good Lord deliver us."

"The funeral's been postponed because of weather," Pauline said. "Betty Ann Pritula announced it." Her voice sounded normal, and the flash of evil had disappeared from her eyes, leaving me to wonder if I'd imagined it.

"I wasn't listening to the radio," I said, apropos of nothing. I'd talked to Elli and Doc, but they must have assumed I'd heard. On the Keweenaw events are always being canceled due to weather, and everyone knew to tune into Betty Ann's program.

"Where's Arvo?"

"On a stranded motorist call."

I was aware that I should have felt a rush of relief. Arvo rescuing a motorist couldn't hurt me. I didn't feel relieved. I felt as if I'd missed a step in the dark. I'd figured it out wrong. It wasn't Arvo who had murdered Liisa and her father. My first reaction was relief that it wasn't Pops's old friend. My second was the realization that I was in this greenhouse, Pauline Maki's sanctuary, alone with a killer.

"Finally figured it out?" Pauline sounded as unconcerned as if she were asking me about a crossword puzzle.

I stared at her. She was almost as familiar in town as her husband, but after twenty some years, she was still seen as an outsider. Even by me.

"It was all a lie," I whispered. "You didn't give her a shower or a cup of tea. I saw the rosebud nightgown in her drawer. The only true thing was the Vicks you rubbed on her chest. The Vicks laced with aconite."

Pauline moved swiftly, easily, to the worktable and scooped up the poisoned medication.

I noticed then, too late, that she was wearing gardening gloves.

CHAPTER TWENTY

"Why?"

On the one hand, I hoped she tell me, because I was curious and needed to know the details, and because I needed some time to regroup and come up with an exit strategy. On the other hand, if she never admitted to it, she might not feel that she had to kill me.

"It's about being an outsider, isn't it?" I babbled, hoping to prime the pump.

Pauline's look was full of contempt and loathing, and I abandoned any hope of clemency. I was pretty sure she was looking forward to killing me. Did Arvo know about his wife's buried hostility? Had he figured out it was she who had slaughtered the girl in their charge?

She seemed to read my thoughts. "He guessed, but he hasn't admitted it, even to himself."

"Denial?"

She gave a harsh, unsettling bark of laughter that, for some reason, helped me calm down a little. At least it indicated she was a human with feelings and not a heartless droid.

"A good one-word summary of our marriage."

The bitterness made my stomach curl.

"If you'd had children . . . ," I heard myself say.

Her scowl was fierce, and I didn't think it was directed at me. It was as if she were glaring into the past.

"It didn't happen, and we told each other it didn't matter. We were a team. We had a mission to save this godforsaken town. Taking in the girl was part of that, and we agreed it would be an adventure; that afterwards, we'd be glad to return to the peace and quiet of our lives."

"It didn't work out like that."

Her eyes looked hollow, her cheeks sallow and her fingers clenched around the jar of poison salve.

"Arvo fell in love."

I felt my jaw drop. I heard the words jump out of my mouth.

"Was he the baby's father?"

The comment, stupid as it was, brought her back to life. Color flamed in her cheeks, and hatred flashed in her eyes.

"He fell in love with being a father. The baby that would make him a grandfather was the final straw."

I didn't fully understand.

"When Arvo told me about the baby, he said it would make both of you grandparents. *Isovanhemmat.*" When she didn't respond, I spoke again. "That wasn't what it felt like to you." Even in her tiny makeshift family, Pauline had been an outsider. "Would it have made a difference if she'd bonded with you the way she did with Arvo?"

I knew the answer even as I spoke. It would never have been enough. Pauline, perhaps deprived of love all her life, had wanted to be everything to Arvo. I wondered if she would have been jealous of her own children.

"He married me because he was fond of me," she said. "And because my family had a lot of money. I knew it, but I couldn't resist his charm and warmth. No one thinks I'm good enough for the town's golden boy, but we were happy enough until she showed up."

Liisa, with her beauty and vulnerability and her attachment to Arvo, had ripped through the curtain of denial, and he'd suddenly discovered that frightening depth of emotion it's possible for one human being to feel towards another. Very much like parenthood, I thought, only, in this case, he hadn't been able to share the feeling with his wife.

"That was the worst of it," she said, reading my mind again. "He was so pleased with himself, like a cat bringing home a dead mouse. He thought Liisa had made me as happy as she made him."

I felt the bitterness and pain that seemed to wrack her thin figure. But there was something I didn't understand.

"You knew she was going to marry and run away with Reid Night Wind. It was you, wasn't it, who kept feeding evidence to Sheriff Clump? Why didn't you just let her go?"

The vacant look was back in her face. This time the words were spoken matter-of-factly.

"She destroyed my life. I had to destroy hers."

There was an ominous sense of purpose in her step as she started toward me. I slipped my hand into my right pocket and wished my fingers would stop shaking.

"And now you feel you have to destroy me, too? How will you explain my death? You can't pin it on Reid. He's still in custody."

"You've got a big mouth, Hatti. You've told people you think it is Arvo. You will turn up dead in Arvo's house, and he will be blamed."

"You'll let him take the fall?" She shrugged. "Do you think he won't fight back?"

"I know he won't. Arvo believes he is a good husband."

I felt a terrifying wave of compassion for both the Makis. I shrugged it off. Pauline might be a devastated wife, but she was also a killer. I froze as thunder exploded overhead, and three feet away, Pauline deftly, expertly unscrewed the top of the Vicks and dipped two gloved fingers into the ointment. By the time she lunged for me, I'd secured my own weapon, prayed I was pointing it in the right direction and pressed my right forefinger down on the nozzle as hard as I could.

Pauline, taken by surprise, shrieked. Her hands flew to her eyes to protect them from the artificial snow at the same time the door burst open behind me. I was aware of Arvo rushing toward his wife even as I heard Jace's hoarse voice calling my name.

"Oh, my God!" Arvo gasped as his wife of twenty years clutched at her throat, then slid to the floor of the greenhouse. "Pauline!"

"She had Vicks on her fingers when she rubbed her eyes." I forced the words out, aware that I'd set her death in motion when I'd sprayed her with artificial snow.

Arvo knelt on the ground, his arms around the woman he hadn't loved enough, and I turned my face into my husband's leather jacket.

CHAPTER TWENTY-ONE

"Tell me again how Aunt Hatti flocked Mrs. Maki," Charlie begged my husband.

Jace, on the loveseat next to me, looked somewhat the worse for wear. There were still blisters and reddened areas on his face from the truck fire, and he was wearing a sling, as he'd dislocated his shoulder breaking down the greenhouse door. My niece was seated cross-legged on the carpeted floor of my parents' parlor next to Reid Night Wind, who was rubbing Larry's tummy. Larry, upside down, his stubby legs in the air, had shut his eyes with ecstasy. Charlie looked as happy as I'd ever seen her, and, even though I knew that, eventually, Reid would break her heart the way Jace had broken mine, I couldn't find it in myself to regret this moment.

After all, what is life, anyway, but a series of moments? This one was happy, and I decided to enjoy it.

" 'The pastures are clothed with flocks, the valleys also are covered over with corn; they shout for joy, they also sing.' " Miss Irene beamed at me.

"Your aunt was very brave," Reid said, after a respectful pause. He winked at me. "In a war of substance versus substance, she picked the right weapon."

I felt Jace's slight shudder.

"She shouldn't have gone to the funeral home by herself."

"I sent you a text," I reminded him.

"I know. I got it while I was waiting for Maki to pick me up with the hearse. I had to tell him what was going on even though I didn't know whether he was in on the murder, too, and that, instead of driving me back to Red Jacket, he'd dump me into Frog Creek."

"I had no way of knowing you were with Arvo."

"I had no way of assisting you."

"Now, now, children," Sofi said. "All's well that ends well. For the record, though, Hatti, I think Jace is right. You were foolish to act on your own."

I couldn't admit that I'd wanted to solve the case by myself. That would sound selfish and egocentric and, well, foolish.

"Anyway, you got there in time to help," I said to Jace.

He shook his head, a bleak look in his gray eyes. "You didn't need me. You rescued yourself."

"Arvo's the one I feel sorry for," Elli said. "He lost a surrogate daughter and a wife. I wonder if he'll ever recover."

I didn't repeat what Pauline had said, that Arvo had guessed at her guilt. There seemed no point in it now that Pauline was dead, and it seemed to me that I'd have had a tough time blowing the whistle on my spouse, too.

"I imagine," Aunt Ianthe said, from her corner on the big sofa, "Arvo had known for some time that Pauline wasn't stable, but he was always loyal."

" 'A true friend is always loyal and a brother is born to help in time of need,' " Miss Irene said. "Psalms 17:17."

"I believe you mean Proverbs, dear," Aunt Ianthe said. "It is so easy to get the two confused."

In spite of the inspirational words I was glad Mom and Pops, exhausted from their trip, had gone upstairs to lie down for awhile. Mom had been upset about what she called my "brush with death." Pops would have been upset to hear everyone talking about his best friend.

"Being a parent went to Arvo's head," Elli said.

I tensed, waiting for Jace to make the point that Liisa had not been Arvo's real daughter. For once, he said nothing.

"I agree," Sofi chimed in. "Arvo should have been more aware of his wife's feelings."

"I imagine he was in denial," Sonya said in her soft voice. "He probably couldn't see anything except his own delight in Liisa."

Miss Irene cocked her head at me like a little bird.

"I have a question, Henrikki. When did you realize that Pauline was the killer?"

I smiled at her. "I was afraid someone would ask me that. The fact is, I didn't know. Even though I found the poisoned Vicks and the backpack in Pauline's greenhouse, I thought Arvo had killed the Pelonens right up until I looked into Pauline's face this afternoon. For the first time she didn't try to hide all that anger, and finally I knew."

"You thought the killer was Arvo Maki, a man you'd known all your life," Reid said, slowly. "You never thought it was me?"

I couldn't tell him how badly I wanted him to be innocent.

"Your brother was a fierce advocate," I said, smiling at the younger man. "He knew your grandfather believed you and that he was never wrong. And then there was the fact that the case against you was so well constructed. It seemed likely that someone had chosen you as the fall guy."

"You didn't really need our help," Elli said, indicating Sofi and Sonya. "I mean, you really figured it out yourself."

"You're totally wrong on that El," I said, shaking my head vigorously. "You got the information from Jake Jussi, Sofi gave me a reason to go back to the funeral home by assigning me a flower delivery, Sonya did that preliminary autopsy, Jace took me up to the mountain to see Reid, Charlie gave me information about Liisa's relationship with the kids at school and Max took me to see Matti Murso." I smiled at the fishing camp owner. I'd had a phone call from Matti earlier. He'd admitted to being the baby's father, which tied up the last loose end. I decided against mentioning that in front of my teenaged niece. No point in giving her any ideas. I glanced at the way her eyes lit up as she spoke with Reid.

"It took a village to solve the murder," Aunt Ianthe said, her knitting needles clicking along. She paused for the inevitable Biblical reverence.

" 'And the Lord did, according to the word of Moses; and the frogs died out of the houses; out of the villages and out of the fields. Exodus 8:13.' "

"I guess it goes to show you can't tell what's going on in someone else's marriage," Elli said, eventually. "Even when they've been married a long time."

"Marriages go bad," Sofi said, darkly, "just like friendships."

Charlie's eyes darted to her mother, and her smile disappeared.

"Not all marriages or friendships," I said, hastily. "Look at Mom and Pops. They're still going strong after more than twenty-five years."

Jace lurched to his feet as if he couldn't sit on the loveseat one more minute.

"I need some air," he said. "I'll take Larry for a walk."

I knew he wanted to be alone. I knew he needed to get away from me. I disregarded that knowledge.

"I'll go with you," I said.

The storm had finally blown itself out. The air was fresh and clear, the stars visible in the dark sky. The recently plowed snow lined the street in piles so high I could barely see from one side of Calumet Street to the other. The curbs and sidewalks were obliterated, and we had to walk in the middle of the street, which, as there was literally no traffic at all, was no problem.

"What will you do now?"

I hadn't meant to question him. I hadn't even meant to talk. I was horrified at the personal nature of the question, the way I'd revealed myself by phrasing it as if there was a chance he'd changed his mind about me. I wanted to tell him to rewind the tape, to forget I'd asked the question, but I figured that would just make things worse. He didn't answer at once. I kept my eyes on the waving tail in front of us and wished I could bore a sudden hole to China.

"I'm going to ask Reid to go back to D.C. with me. He needs something to do, and I think he'll catch on quickly as office manager."

My old job. I guess that told me everything I wanted to know.

Jace stopped suddenly and turned to me.

"You've grown beyond that job, Hatti. I think it's time you went back to law school."

"I'm not interested in law school."

"You interested in a baby?"

"What?"

He shrugged. "You're not getting any younger."

I was furious. "You have some nerve, Jace Night Wind. You dump me without explanation, ignore me for a year, then insult me when we bump into each other."

"It's not a bump into. I came out here on purpose to talk to you."

I decided to ignore the untruth in that statement. I gazed at him steadily. "Then talk."

He looked beyond me at the jagged drifts that made Calumet Street look like a moonscape.

"I apologize for last year. I went off the deep end in a way that was completely unfair to you. I've missed you like hell, Umlaut. I want you to come home with me."

I'd waited a long time for that apology. It seemed heartfelt and sincere, and I wondered why it didn't make me happy.

"Is that all?"

"Pretty much."

I shook my head. "Why'd you do it, Jace?"

I could almost hear his internal sigh. My husband wasn't exactly a genius at communication, and he liked talking about his feelings about as much as he liked the prospect of a root canal.

"You and I feel differently about family," he said. "Yours is important to you."

He paused when I shook my head.

"Reid is important to you, important enough that you came back to the Keweenaw to try to save his hide. Your grandfather's important, too."

Jace scowled. "I'm talking about you, Hatti. Your sister's family means everything to you. So do your folks." I wondered if it was my imagination that he'd tripped over that last word. "Last year I discovered something that would have divided you from them forever if you'd stayed with me."

"What?"

He didn't answer the question. "I didn't think it was fair to make you choose."

"You mean you didn't want to see me choose them over you?"

I'd never seen Jace flush before. Geez Louise, with his deeply tanned skin I wasn't sure he could flush.

"When I stopped at the Copper Eagle, I found my birth certificate in a shoebox. It was the first time I'd seen the name of my natural father."

"Who was it?" I'd planned to maintain a dignified silence, but my curiosity got the better of me.

"The name on the certificate was Carl Lehtinen."

"Pops?" I stared at him for a long moment while my mind ran over everything I knew about Jace's childhood. His mother, pregnant and abandoned at fifteen, had run north to a Canadian rez, where she and her illegitimate half-Ojibwe son were not accepted. His mother had drunk too much, partied too much and wound up selling her body for booze while he, Jace, had been forced to steal enough food to keep them alive. How much it must have hurt to discover that the man who should have protected Miriam Night Wind and her son had, instead, spent his life providing for another woman and raising her children in a house filled with kindness and love.

It wasn't true, though.

"Pops can't be your father," I said, gently. "I know him. He wouldn't have left your mother unprotected. Not even when he was a young man."

"He probably never knew she was pregnant."

I held his gaze. "He'd have known if there was a chance. He wouldn't have abandoned her. Or you."

Jace's gray eyes narrowed.

"Are you saying my mother lied?"

I shook my head again. I wanted to tell him I just knew about Pops, the same way I'd known that Jace was the only man for me. It seemed like an inappropriate argument under the circumstances and a little beside the point.

"Come with me," I said, taking his hand. "Let's go talk to him."

CHAPTER TWENTY-TWO

My folks were up, bustling around, serving food and drinks, and reveling in being home again after being away for a month. I held onto Jace's wrist as if he were a toddler ready to escape at the first opportunity, signaled Pops and a few minutes later the three of us were settled into the comfortable furniture in his study. It seemed odd to think that it was only a few hours ago that I'd sat in the easy chair reading about the medieval monk and the aconite poisoning. Pops looked so familiar there, so right.

We sat in silence for a minute or two, half listening to the bursts of laughter that reached us from the kitchen on the other side of the wall. Pops settled against the backrest while Jace, next to me on the leather sofa, leaned forward, his elbows on his thighs, his hands between them. He reminded me of a distance runner waiting for the starting gun. I felt like an untrained hostage negotiator, but someone had to get the ball rolling. I jumped in with both feet and no life jacket.

"Jace found his birth certificate out at Chief Joseph's last year," I told Pops. "Your name is listed as his father."

I didn't defend him the way I had outdoors. Pops knew how I felt about him.

His blue eyes looked weary, but they filled with compassion. He spoke gently.

"I knew your mama before you were born. It was the summer after I'd finished college, and I hired on with a work crew to install plumbing on the rez. The project had to be done in a short amount of time, so families let us workers sleep at their homes so we didn't have to waste time driving back and forth to our own homes all over the Keweenaw.

"The crew chief warned us not to take advantage of the local girls, but there were parties and campfires, and there was beer. Your mama was the prettiest girl, but she was very young, and, well, she was wild. Too wild. I suspected, but I didn't know. Not until now."

Jace's fingers had closed into fists, and I could see a muscle twitch in his clenched jaw.

"It wasn't me, son. Miriam Night Wind flirted with all of us, but everybody knew she really only had eyes for one young man. I knew he'd held out for awhile." He shook his head. "It seems he lost the battle." Pops seemed to study Jace's face. "If I'd met you before today I might have seen it. You have that same something. Charm, I suppose."

"You know who Jace's father is?"

Pops nodded without looking at me. "He's a good man, son, but even a good man makes mistakes."

There weren't many men in Red Jacket who were fatally attractive to women, and it wasn't hard to figure out who'd seduced or succumbed to Miriam Night Wind. Jace's jaw was clenched so hard I was afraid he'd shatter his teeth, and I could tell by the way he looked at Pops that he'd figured it out, too.

"Arvo," I breathed.

Jace focused on Pops's kindly face.

"Why would my mother lie?"

"I don't know. They were both underage. She may have been trying to protect him. Or, she may have been trying to protect herself. He couldn't have married her. She was only fifteen."

"She may have decided to stir up trouble on a whim," Jace said, bitterly. "It would have been like her."

Because Arvo had been weak, Jace had lost out on his childhood, and because Miriam Night Wind had liked to stir up trouble, Jace and I had lost out on our marriage. I wanted to cry.

Pops left us alone, and, for awhile, we just sat in the study, half listening to the sounds in the rest of the house. It was a comfortable silence, though. A fly on the wall would have guessed we'd been married a long time and had passed the point of needing to talk. But flies have never been celebrated for their insight, and the opposite was true.

We needed to talk. We just couldn't seem to find the words.

"I need to go home."

I checked my watch and gaped at my sister. "It's only ten o'clock. I thought we were going to ring in the new year with a sauna and a roll in the snow."

"I'm not six, Hatti."

It was, of course, a ridiculous excuse. The New Year's Eve sauna is a dearly held tradition in our culture and has nothing to do with age, but I didn't argue. I'd heard the edge in Sofi's voice and figured she was fretting about something. I figured, too, she'd tell me what it was when she wanted me to know.

The mood ticked down after Sofi left. The three of us sprawled on Elli's carefully rehabilitated Victorian furniture like slugs on a sidewalk. It may have been Sofi's early departure, or it may have been because we were almost sick from stuffing our faces with crackers and brie, *joulutorttu* and the leftover Christmas fudge. Or it may have been that we'd polished off all several bottles of *Painted Turtle,* a locally bottled sweet wine composed of blackberries, cloudberries, white grapes, honey and bananas.

I was half asleep when Sonya asked me about Jace.

"I thought you'd be going back to D.C.," she said. "But don't tell us about it if you don't want to."

I hadn't wanted to talk, which was uncharacteristic of me. I kept second-guessing my decision—and his—and I was tired of hurting. I just wanted to move forward with my life.

"He asked me to go back with him, and I asked him to stay here. We were at an impasse."

Elli sat up. "You asked him to stay here? What about his job?"

It was a fair question and one Jace had asked, too.

I sat up, too. "Jace proved last year that his hatred of his father is stronger than his feelings for me. The same thing could happen again if he doesn't make his peace with Arvo."

"You want him to stay on the Keweenaw for his own good," Sonya said, slowly.

"And because his unconscious feelings could sabotage your marriage again," Elli added, with admirable perception.

"And because I belong here. This is my home."

The statement had the merit of being partly true.

We talked about the concept of home and the nature of our small closed community. We recalled the high points of our recent investigation, and we speculated on the secrets in every individual and every marriage. It was nearly midnight when we realized the evening—and the year—were nearly at an end.

"I wonder," Sonya said, getting to her feet, "what the new year holds for us."

"There's one way to find out," Elli said, jumping to her feet. Sonya and I followed her into the kitchen.

"What's going on?" the Navajo midwife asked, as we watched Elli drag Grandma Risto's tin wash basin out of a cupboard.

"Valuteos läkkipelti."

Sonya's dark eyes widened. "That sounds dangerous."

"It's a kind of fortune-telling," I said. "You melt tin and read your future in the shape." I wasn't certain I wanted to participate. What if I got a heart or some other symbol of love? I didn't want to be reminded of what I'd lost or of my part in the losing. I reminded myself it was just a game.

Elli filled the basin with ice and cold water while I boiled more water in the tea kettle and poured it into a smaller pan. We set both vessels on the kitchen table, and Elli handed us each a horseshoe charm.

"It isn't really tin," Elli explained. "These days we use an alloy. It just works better. This one," she said, tossing a horseshoe into the hot water, "is for Sofi." She used a long-handled spoon to transfer the melted charm into the basin. I couldn't help remembering the old proverb about needing a long spoon to sup with the devil. I turned off the overhead light and lit a bayberry candle, which I held at an angle that cast a shadow onto the side of the basin.

"It's a rabbit," Sonya said. "See the ears and the little cotton tail?"

"Undeniably a rabbit," Elli agreed. I felt my heart sink.

"I'm guessing it means fertility," Sonya said.

"Or bankruptcy," I said. "Let's not mention this to Sofe. Go ahead, Elli."

My cousin's shape was as clear as the rabbit, and I was startled when she failed to read it.

"A parallelogram," she said.

"Somehow, I don't think the pagan gods knew about high school geometry," I murmured. "Look at it from this angle." Elli shifted her position and gasped.

"It's a diamond."

"Does that mean you'll be getting engaged?" Sonya asked.

"Or I might come into some money," Elli said. "A diamond represents wealth, too."

It didn't. My cousin, normally a stickler for tradition, was willing to subvert the rules, and I thought I knew why. She seldom spoke about her single status, probably because she knew it was unlikely to change. Red Jacket was not exactly a dating mecca, since the young people who stuck around were usually married in their teens. It might have happened to Elli. We all thought it would happen, but it hadn't. Elli had thrown herself into the transformation of the Leaping Deer. She never talked about marriage for herself.

A moment later we peered at Sonya's tin.

"It looks like a steak knife," she said.

I caught Elli's eye. "A knife symbolizes cutting," I said, "like cutting off dead wood or the past."

Sonya's well-shaped lips tightened into a straight line for a fraction of a second, and then she grinned.

"A fresh start. Exactly what I'd have chosen for myself. Your turn, Hatti."

I knew exactly what to expect in the coming year. I'd get back to my shop, straighten out the inventory, place orders and resume my neglected knitting blog. It would be considerably less exciting than investigating a murder, so I wasn't all that surprised when my charm turned into a shapeless blob.

"Try again," said Elli, who was apparently taking her new rule-breaking role seriously.

"No, thanks. A blob suits me just fine."

"Hold on," Sonya said, peering into the basin. "It's still changing. I see," she paused, "well, you'll think I'm crazy."

"A skull and crossbones." Elli and I spoke at the same time. "Violent death," she whispered.

"Maybe it will change again," Sonya suggested. We hovered around the basin like Macbeth's three weird sisters inspecting their brew. My cellphone's ringtone sent a jolt through my heart. I knew it was Jace. Had he changed his mind, or would he just wish me a Happy New Year? I told myself to be cool.

"*Onnellista Uutta Vuotta,*" I said, somewhat breathlessly.

"Happy New Year!"

There was a pause and then a deep, humorless voice.

"I hope yours is starting out better than mine."

"Lars." I fought a dismaying sense of disappointment. "What's up? Where are you?"

"Jail."

I closed my eyes. He'd been drinking.

"I'll come and get you. What's the bail?"

"This isn't a DUI, Squirt. I'm here for the duration."

I didn't understand. "Duration of what?"

"Until Clump finds enough evidence to formally arrest me."

"I don't understand."

"It's simple enough." I pictured his characteristic shrug. "When I got home tonight there was a girl in my bed. A dead girl."

"Why? How? Who?"

"I don't know why. I don't know the 'how' yet, either. I do know the 'who.' She is—or was—a waitress at the Black Fly in Chassell. Her name's Cricket Koski."

I didn't know what to say. Lars's one-night stand with the woman my sister refers to as "insect girl" was the final straw for my sister's tottering marriage.

"I know it looks bad," he said, and I knew he wasn't referring to his legal problems. "I have no idea how she wound up in my cabin, much less how she died. But I need to find out, and I can't do it from here."

"I'll help," I heard myself say.

"I figured you would. Come by in the morning. Early."

I hung up and reported what I'd heard.

"Thank goodness Sofi isn't here," Elli said. I sent her a bleak look. This wasn't something we could hide from my sister or anyone else.

"It's freaky," Sonya pointed out. "I mean, we just got that

fortune about a violent death."

I stared at her. "It was murder, wasn't it? It must have been." I was a little ashamed of the sudden spurt of adrenaline.

"This time it will be up to your dad or the sheriff to solve the crime," Elli said, but I didn't mistake the flash of eagerness in her pixie-ish face. The three of us exchanged a significant look that had nothing to do with my reply.

"Of course."

ABOUT THE AUTHOR

Ann Yost is a University of Michigan grad, a onetime newspaper reporter, a humor columnist and the author of six romantic mysteries: *About a Baby, He Loves Lucy, Eye of the Tiger Lily, The Earl That I Marry, For Better or Hearse* and *That Voodoo That You Do.*

Ann lives with her husband, an Associated Press reporter, in northern Virginia. She spends her non-writing time hanging out with pets and friends, reading mysteries and visiting family in Michigan, New York and Boston. She would love to hear from you at www.annyost.com.